1047536

A Costly Mistake

"I've never seen that necklace before," I said. "It's amazing!"

Mrs. Mahoney fingered it wistfully. "It's a real treasure. It's old as old can be. It belonged to Cornelius's mother, but she used to say that it dates back to the days of Louis the Fourteenth in France!" She held up the gem to the light. "It's the real thing—an emerald."

"And you're wearing it?" Ned visibly gulped.

Mrs. Mahoney looked sheepish. "I shouldn't be. It *is* insured, but the fastening isn't as secure as it should be. I keep meaning to bring it to Dave's Jewels and Gems to have him put on a safety chain. But since I seldom wear it, I never get around to fixing it."

"You shouldn't wait on that sort of thing," Ned remarked. "It would be a pity to lose it."

NANCY DREW
girl detective™

Available from Aladdin Paperbacks

NANCY DREW

DREW

girl detective ™

#11

Riverboat Ruse

Nancy Drew
75th
ANNIVERSARY

CAROLYN KEENE

Aladdin Paperbacks
New York   London   Toronto   Sydney

This book is a work of fiction. Any references to historical events, real people, or real locales are used fictitiously. Other names, characters, places, and incidents are the product of the author's imagination, and any resemblance to actual events or locales or persons, living or dead, is entirely coincidental.

ALADDIN PAPERBACKS
An imprint of Simon & Schuster Children's Publishing Division
1230 Avenue of the Americas, New York, NY 10020
Copyright © 2005 by Simon and Schuster, Inc.
All rights reserved, including the right of
reproduction in whole or in part in any form.
ALADDIN PAPERBACKS, NANCY DREW, and colophon are registered trademarks of Simon & Schuster, Inc.
NANCY DREW: GIRL DETECTIVE is a trademark of Simon & Schuster, Inc.
Manufactured in the United States of America
First Aladdin Paperbacks edition May 2005
10 9 8 7 6 5 4 3 2
Library of Congress Control Number 2004108764
ISBN 0-689-87335-2

Contents

A Curious Tale

I was midway through speed-dialing my boyfriend, Ned, on my cell phone when my best friend Bess Marvin grabbed my sleeve. "Nancy, look! It's here."

I totally forgot about my call. Sure enough, the ship was rounding the bend in the river just south of the bluffs in Riverside Park. As it drew closer, I was able to read the bold, black print on its side: THE MAGNOLIA BELLE. Its decks were tiered like a white wedding cake, and it gleamed in the bright morning light. The handful of local residents gathered on the dock to witness the arrival of the latest attraction in our city's Seventy-fifth Midsummer Muskoka River Festival began to cheer.

"Finally," George Fayne remarked. George is my

other best friend, and Bess's cousin. "It's sure a slow mover."

"But it's almost here now!" Bess bounced a little on her toes. Though Bess and George are first cousins and best friends, they have two completely different outlooks on life: Bess is an incurable optimist, while George is a glass-half-empty sort of person.

Today, however, they were equally eager to greet the *Magnolia Belle*. Bess had landed a two-week job as an intern with the ship's maintenance crew and had to check in. George was there on her mother's behalf. Her mom's catering business had snared the contract for the big event—the Whodunit Dinner and the overnight cruise between River Heights and Sutter's Cove.

The cruise was a fund-raiser for several charitable organizations in River Heights. About forty of our city's most affluent citizens had purchased tickets for the overnight luxury journey. I was lucky that my dad had bought two tickets for the event. At the last minute he learned that he couldn't be in town for the cruise— business called—but he told me to invite Ned.

Ned. Where was he?

I had just finished leaving him a message when I heard a familiar voice behind me. "Would you look at that!" The voice belonged to one of my good friends from town, Luther Eldridge. He's an expert on the history of River Heights and knows all sorts of trivia about the area.

"Luther!" I greeted him. "I don't have to ask why *you're* here. How long has it been since a riverboat docked in River Heights?"

Luther didn't even pretend to think about it. "Sixty-two years, four months, and three days to the day."

"But I bet the last one was bigger." Bess sounded disappointed. "This isn't half as big as the ones George showed us online the other night."

Luther and I took a good look at the boat. Bess was right. The image of the paddleboat we saw online was as large as a small cruise ship. This riverboat was probably half that size. But it was still grand and beautiful, and I couldn't wait to board her.

The *Magnolia Belle*'s big red paddle wheel was at the rear of the boat, churning up a frothy wake. Plumes of white steam rose from the two black smokestacks on either side of the wheelhouse. But though the riverboat looked like something from another century, I noticed a radar antenna on top of the wheelhouse slowly sweeping the sky.

"What's making the boat go?" George asked as the riverboat docked.

"Superheated water in a boiler," Bess and Luther answered in unison. Luther laughed, then made a gesture toward Bess. "I'll let the mechanical expert explain."

Bess shook her head. "Let's wait to get the real story from one of the pros on the boat."

Just then the boat finished docking, and people began descending the gangplank.

"That guy's an old salt if I've ever seen one. I bet he's the captain." Luther pointed to a stocky man wearing navy blue trousers who was headed for the pier. He looked a bit older than my dad. His white cap was pushed back over a shock of thick, faded blond hair. His round face was beet red as he argued furiously with a man who followed him down onto the pier. An image of a steamboat and the words *Magnolia Belle* decorated his shirt.

"He sure looks *steamed* over something," George quipped.

Bess and I cringed over George's pun. But she was right about the "old salt's" mood. Both men were having what was at the very least an extremely heated conversation. The other man looked calmer—and he bore an uncanny resemblance to Mark Twain. He had a bushy white mustache, and longish white hair poked out from beneath his old-fashioned pale straw hat.

The Mark Twain look-alike spotted us first. He put a restraining hand on the captain's arm, and immediately the argument stopped. As the captain shifted his gaze toward us, his angry expression swiftly morphed to a welcoming smile. The other man hurried back up the gangplank and disappeared into the ship.

The captain greeted us with a deep Southern drawl. "I didn't expect such a welcoming committee." He seemed pleasant enough as he stretched out a hand to Luther, then to me and my friends. But his eyes were small and shrewd, and seemed at odds with his smile.

"Captain Mike Jones here. Just call me Captain Mike."

"This is Luther Eldridge, our unofficial town historian. I'm Nancy Drew, and these are my friends Bess Marvin and George Fayne."

Captain Mike turned to George first. "You're one of the Faynes from Ready, Set, Eat!, the catering company?"

George nodded. "I work part-time for my mother, Louise. She sent me to scope out the galley."

Captain Mike waved toward the lower deck of the ship. A couple of guys were hanging over the railing, staring in our direction. One was tall and skinny. The other, even from this distance, looked like a well-built hunk. "Ken!" the captain shouted. "Come down here."

A moment later the skinny guy joined us. "Hi, I'm Ken Perkins," he said.

"Ken's one of our waiters," the captain told George.

5

"He'll show you the galley, the food-storage facilities, and of course, cabins for you and your mother."

"Hi!" another voice chimed in. We all turned around. The hunk had just walked up. He had dark blond hair and amazing blue eyes. He seemed to light up at the sight of Bess.

Surprise, surprise!

"And this," the captain said, sounding decidedly less enthusiastic, "is my nephew, Dylan."

"Oh, Dylan Jones," Bess remarked. "I think I'm supposed to be working with you. I'm Bess Marvin."

Dylan just gaped at Bess. "*You're* the intern?"

George and I exchanged a quick glance. When guys first meet Bess, they always take her for pretty and helpless—and then get the shock of their lives. Bess can fix cars and solder plumbing pipes. She shops for tools with the same relish with which she hits stores like Boutique and Beyond at the mall. Not your average pretty blonde.

Bess smothered a smile. "Yeah." She pulled an envelope out of her bag, reached across Dylan, and handed it to the captain. "Here's my acceptance letter."

Captain Mike looked at the letter. "Right. You're the one who's a certified carpenter. I'm impressed. Maybe you can teach Dylan something!" From his tone I wasn't sure he was joking. Neither was Dylan. He winced.

6

Bess looked puzzled. "Oh, no. I'm the one here to learn," she protested. "I certainly don't know a thing about steamboats . . . except what I've read."

"Time to cure that!" the captain said to Bess. "Dylan, show our new intern the engineering department, the boiler room, the ship's workshop, and then where she'll be bunking." He turned to Luther and me and added, "I bet the town historian—official or not—would like to tour the boat. Come on, you two. I'll show you the ropes."

While Ken led George directly to the galley, Bess and Dylan went below. Luther and I followed the captain. We learned that the *Magnolia Belle* was a scaled-down version of some of the cruise-ship-class riverboats that used to supply the shores of the Mississippi and Ohio Rivers. It had only three passenger decks, with sixty cabins.

As soon as we reached the Main Deck, Captain Mike took us to the back of the boat. "This is the paddle wheel," he pointed out. "Because it's attached to the back—or stern—of the boat, this kind of vessel is called a stern-wheeler."

"As I recall," Luther contributed, "stern-wheelers came along and gradually replaced side-wheelers."

"What's a side-wheeler?" I asked.

"They were the first type of riverboats and had two paddles, one on the port, or left side of the ship, and one on the starboard, or right side of the ship," the captain explained.

Narrow stairs led from deck to deck on the outside of the ship. Inside, the captain told us, there were regular staircases, and an elevator for passengers who were unable to climb stairs easily.

A set of double doors led to the dining room. I could see through the glass that a stage was set up, and actors were still rehearsing for that night's performance.

As we headed up past the Plantation Deck, to the Star Deck and Observation Lounge, I noticed a lifeboat suspended by ropes off the side of the ship toward the bow of the Main Deck. It was covered with a black tarp. "Do you ever need that boat?" I asked him.

"No, thank goodness. Generally, river cruises are pretty quiet. We watch for weather. We just cancel if a bad storm is predicted."

"So it's not like the old days, when there were boiler explosions and ships were caught on snags," Luther commented.

The captain laughed. "No way. Believe me, all the kinks were worked out of steam engines some time ago. We undergo a topside Coast Guard inspection once a year, and every two years there's a bottom inspection—when the hull and general structure is checked out.

"We follow all navigational rules. We have a good supply of life jackets. And you'll see life preservers on every deck, just in case someone falls in the river. Now that *has* happened once or twice." Captain Mike chuckled. "Mainly kids leaning too far over the rails. No one ever got hurt, though."

"They could if they fell near that paddle wheel," Luther noted.

The captain frowned. "True. Even though we seldom travel more than five miles an hour, it's heavy, and churns up the water. As for the lifeboats—they're not mandatory, but I like the idea of them."

"You've got more than one?" I asked as we mounted the last of the steps leading to the top deck.

"Yeah, two. The life jackets are all stowed under those benches along the railings and in other places on the ship."

Captain Mike held open the door leading into the Observation Lounge. I walked in first, followed by Luther. The wood-paneled lounge had plenty of easy chairs. Card tables sat catty-corner along the far wall. Another wall held a three-foot-high bookshelf filled with all sorts of reading material. Hung above the shelf were framed maps and prints. A wooden flat file jutted out from beneath one of the windows. Someone had spread out a map on top.

Luther made a beeline for the framed prints. He

moved from one to another, studying them. Suddenly he let out a low impressed whistle. "Captain Mike, do you realize what you have here?"

The captain shook his head. I hurried over to Luther, curious. He tapped the glass of the framed print. "This is the *Lucinda Lu*."

"Didn't she sink or something?" the captain asked.

"I'd say so!" Luther exclaimed. "She went down in local history as the biggest steamboat disaster ever on the Muskoka River."

"She sank around here?" The captain seemed surprised.

"A few months ago I came across some old articles about the disaster. It was supposed to be an accident, but . . ." Luther paused for effect and looked at me and winked. "Nancy will love this. It turns out the accident was suspicious because it happened just as the boat was passing Stony Lonesome Island just a few miles up from River Heights—twenty-four hours after a bank heist in Willow Bend, a little farther downstream."

"You mean the crooks somehow engineered an explosion?" I asked.

"No one ever knew for sure—but lots of people died, and no one ever learned the truth or found the loot."

2

Sleight of Hand

"Is this story for real—or some kind of legend?" The captain sounded skeptical.

Luther grinned. "I found the account in the town archives a while back. I've been meaning to take a trip to Stony Lonesome Island ever since, but haven't gotten around to it. Haven't been there since I went on a high-school picnic."

"You didn't know that the *Lucinda Lu* disaster happened on this stretch of river?" I asked the captain.

He shook his head.

I was surprised. "I'd think since you've sailed the Muskoka before, you'd know all about it." Then it occurred to me that he'd never actually told me he'd sailed the river. "That's right, isn't it?"

"Ah," he said, pushing back his hat. "I've never

11

sailed this river before. It was actually my first mate's idea to book some events along the Muskoka this summer. He's familiar with the channels, and I was game for some new scenery." Turning back to Luther, he said, "I'm real curious about this story. You say they never found the dough?"

"Nope . . . at least not to anyone's knowledge," Luther replied. "Back in the eighteen seventies when this happened, even after the authorities combed the caves on the island, all sorts of folks would boat out there and explore those caves. If anyone stashed stolen money there, it's long gone."

"If the robbers engineered that disaster, they must have had accomplices on the island who came back for the money later," I surmised.

The captain glanced sharply at me. "Smart thinking."

He went over to the flat file and leaned over the map. "Luther," he said after studying it a moment. "It looks like the channels are deep enough on one side of the island for this ship to travel."

Luther hooked his fingers in his belt loops and shrugged. "Can't say I know much about the depth of the river . . . just that shoals change depending on whether we've had enough rain."

"No problem this year," the captain said, then eyeballed Luther. "How'd you like a free berth on the cruise tonight?"

"Are you inviting me to the Whodunit Dinner?" Luther looked flabbergasted.

"Sure! And since there's a full moon, and we're definitely going to pass Stony Lonesome Island tonight, we could have a little side excursion. We can use the lifeboats. You could give a lecture—"

"Hey, if you've got some good flashlights and lanterns," Luther interrupted, "I can even show people the caves!"

I could see Luther was thrilled at the prospect.

The captain looked doubtful. "Are they safe?"

"Safe *and* shallow," Luther told him.

"No bears, or . . ."

I tried not to laugh. "Not for a long time, Captain Mike. Not much wildlife of that sort in River Heights. No one even goes to the island much these days. High-school kids row out there for picnics. But I doubt anyone hangs out there much at night. The river's a bit tricky."

"I'd say so—the charts indicate the Muskoka has some narrow, windy channels. Still, it sounds like a wonderful plan, Luther. I bet I'm not the only one who'd love to hear how the island got its name. And maybe you could spice up the evening by telling us what you know about the history of the *Lucinda Lu*."

Luther slapped his hand into Captain Mike's, sealing the deal.

"The *Magnolia Belle* is one classy dame!" George was practically oozing enthusiasm as I drove her back down to Chestnut Street, to her mother's office. After our tour Luther had gone home to pack his overnight bag, and I hooked up with George. "It's even got wireless Internet connections!"

"Great—you can get online with your laptop when you have time," I said as I parked in front of the catering establishment.

"Will you be just helping in the kitchen or waiting tables?" I asked.

"Just working the kitchen," George answered, tucking her handheld in the front compartment of her knapsack. "The *Belle's* got four permanent waiters. Three guys—you met Ken earlier—and one woman. She looks like she'll be fun to work with."

"So maybe you won't have to fill in," I said, hoping George could hang out at the table where my dad had gotten seats.

George shrugged. "Don't know. I'll have to dress for the occasion just in case," she added, making a face. "You know, the usual—black pants, white blouse, and polished shoes." George hates dressing up and thinks paying too much attention to clothes is a waste of time.

She climbed out of the car. "If you're not busy this afternoon, maybe you could give me a hand. I need to cart some equipment back to the boat. My car's acting up again, and Mom will need the company van."

We agreed to meet around two, and I headed home. I still needed to firm up plans with Ned. We'd be sharing Mrs. Mahoney's table. Agnes Mahoney is one of the wealthiest people in River Heights, and a good client of my father's. We've become friends over the years. I drop in to visit her now and then for afternoon tea. She's a classy woman.

When I tried Ned's home phone, his mother told me he was still volunteering at Camp Muskoka, a reading-and-sports day camp for disadvantaged kids. Mrs. Nickerson told me that Ned would be bringing his campers down to the riverfront to see the *Magnolia Belle,* and suggested I catch up with him there.

I checked my watch and realized I still had to pick out my outfit for the evening and pack a change of clothes for the next day. I finally settled on a pair of low-rise brown pants and a new brown-and-blue-striped silk shirt that Bess had made me buy last week at the mall. She said the colors went well with my reddish blond hair and brought out the blue in my eyes. It was dressy enough for the dinner, but comfortable enough in case Luther's island side trip actually panned out.

By the time I finished packing, Hannah, our housekeeper, had left for the store. So I wrote her a note, then threw a blue hoodie in the backseat of my car and headed off to pick up George at Ready, Set, Eat!

The marina was jammed when we arrived. It seemed as if half of River Heights had turned up to check out the *Magnolia Belle*. People milled around the pier while a member of the crew handed out promotional flyers and answered questions. Captain Mike had told us that after the cruise the steamboat would be open for public tours.

I helped George unload the catering gear at the end of the pier, then left to park the car. When I returned, George was talking to Ned. She had commandeered a wheeled cart and piled her catering supplies inside. She and Ned were standing next to Scalawags, Joe Renaldi's snack shop on the pier. Ned had one eye on George, and the other on the line of kids waiting to buy ice cream. All the kids wore matching red T-shirts with the Camp Muskoka logo printed on the back

"Hey!" Ned said as I walked up.

"You all set for tonight?" I asked after a quick kiss hello.

Ned shook his head. "Not yet. Unfortunately I won't have time to pick you up at home. I've got to get these kids back to camp, and then change and get my overnight bag. We'll have to meet on the boat."

"That sounds fine," I said. "You're going to love the boat."

"I can't wait to board it," Ned said. "It looks like something out of Mark Twain. I tried to get the kids interested in reading *Tom Sawyer*. It didn't work."

"Because you didn't resort to *bribery*," George pointed out. She gestured toward the boat. At the foot of the gangplank a tall girl was standing in the midst of a crowd of young campers. She dug into a large tote bag and pulled out some toys. From where I stood, I couldn't quite see what they were.

"I'd better check this out," Ned said, and started down the pier.

I followed, while George trailed behind with her cart full of supplies. Up close I saw the girl was beautiful, with huge, dark eyes fringed by dark lashes. I watched as she spotted Ned and treated him to a big smile. Ned smiled back. I'm not usually the possessive type, but at that moment I found myself wishing that he wasn't so good-looking. Or at least that he wasn't the friendliest guy in town. "One of the actresses," I guessed.

"Her?" George scoffed. "No way. She's one of the waiters." George made a megaphone of her hands and shouted, "Hey, Hillary! Over here. I want you to meet someone."

Hillary looked right past me toward Ned, and

now I really felt jealous. She loped gracefully toward us. She moved with the ease of a dancer or athlete. "Hi!" she said, reaching out to shake Ned's hand. "Hillary Duval here."

George's dark eyebrows arched up, indicating that my boyfriend-stealing radar wasn't malfunctioning. "This is Ned Nickerson, and this is Nancy Drew. She's the person I told you about."

"You're George's best friend." Hillary's smile seemed genuine enough. When she shook my hand, I noticed her fingers were slender and unusually long. "George said you'll be on the cruise."

Ned put his arm around my shoulder and gave me a peck on the cheek. "Yeah, and she snared me a seat too." I watched Hillary's face. She took in Ned's gesture and looked briefly disappointed. Then the moment passed.

Or rather, got interrupted.

"I HATE YOU!" a shrill, childish voice shrieked.

Ned groaned. "*Now* what?" He hurried over to the line of campers. A girl was screaming at a boy. Between them, on the pier, lay the remains of a strawberry ice-cream cone. "Lauren, what happened?" he asked.

"Luis hit me," she blubbered. "It fell."

"Luis, hitting isn't nice. Lauren, we'll get you another cone," Ned said, digging in his pocket. From the dismayed expression on his face, I realized that he

18

probably had forgotten his wallet. Ned was always forgetting his wallet. Bess told me it was one of the reasons we made a good couple: I tend to forget things too.

Before Lauren had time to notice Ned's gesture, Hillary stooped down in front of her. "Hey, Lauren, want to see something really, really cool?"

Lauren shook her head and blubbered some more.

Hillary tossed her mane of hair back from her face and put her hand behind Lauren's ear. She pulled her hand back, opened her fist, and was holding a dollar bill.

Lauren's tears stopped midsob. "How—how'd you do that?"

Frankly, I wanted to know myself.

"That's a pretty useful trick," Ned remarked. He supplemented the dollar with pocket change, and Lauren promptly went back to Scalawags.

Hillary shrugged off the compliment. "Had a roomie in college who loved magic when she was a kid. She taught me a couple of tricks. They come in handy sometimes."

"I thought magicians weren't supposed to give away the secrets of their tricks," George commented in her usual blunt way.

"Who gave anything away?" Hillary said, smiling wryly. "Anyway, magicians don't," Hillary said. "But I doubt those rules really apply to kids learning tricks from magic hobby kits." Hillary seemed to notice George's cart for the first time. "I know an even better trick to make that heap of stuff disappear. It's called 'helping hands.'"

Ned touched my arm. "Gotta run. See you later."

"If you need to reach me, call my cell. I won't be going home again," I told him. "I've got everything with me. I'll change for dinner here. The boat leaves at seven sharp," I reminded him.

George, Hillary, and I were still sorting out George's gear on the pier when Bess marched up. She was toting plastic shopping bags from Garber's Hardware.

"Now *that's* not the picture of a happy camper," George remarked under her breath.

Indeed, Bess looked beyond annoyed.

"What happened?" I asked as she drew near.

Bess just shrugged. "Nothing." She paused, then rolled her eyes. "That's just it—*nothing*. I've been working on this boat about five hours already, and all I've done is run errands." She plunked the bags down on the pier and began ticking points off on her fingers. "I've gone twice to Mugged for lattes; I've inventoried the contents of three different tool boxes; I'm back just now from my third trip to the hardware store." She heaved a huge sigh. "This job was advertised as 'Mechanic's Intern.' Not 'Gofer.'"

Hillary overheard Bess's comment and laughed.

"Not to worry. If you're working alongside Dylan, you're going to have more than your share of work to do. Believe me."

"But Dylan's the one who's sending me on all these errands," Bess protested.

"Give it time. You'll see," Hillary added mysteriously. Then she shouldered two of George's canvas totes and led the way onto the *Magnolia Belle*.

The dining-room doors were open, and a slightly raised stage spanned one side of the elegantly decorated chamber. Chairs were still upended on tables, and one of the crew was running a vacuum cleaner over the carpet. But as we passed through to the kitchen, my attention was riveted to the stage. The guy who looked like Mark Twain was standing near the footlights, waving a script at a thin-faced woman. She was probably in her late forties or early fifties. Her hair was a brownish red, and she was striking, with a haunted, faded sort of beauty. But she looked as if she was about to burst into tears.

"Cassidy, you've got to pull yourself together. The performance is in a few hours, and you're blowing your lines." I could tell from the man's voice he was quickly losing patience.

"Two pages are missing from my copy of the script," she cried, a note of hysteria in her voice. "Someone or *something* on this cursed ship has it in for me!"

3

Jinxed

Cassidy ran down the steps leading from the stage, then dashed across the dining room. As she passed I saw that she was crying.

The man hurried after her. "Cassidy, come back!" he called. "I'm sorry I lost it back there."

She was already halfway up the stairs that led to the next deck, when she stopped and turned. "Forget it!" she said with a sob, then threw the script at the man.

"You're overreacting," he told her, nimbly ducking and retrieving the script.

"Am I?" she asked, her bottom lip trembling. "First the locket, now this. Find yourself another leading lady. I can't take this anymore. Everything about this gig is jinxed!"

With that she bolted up the rest of the steps. A

moment later I heard a door slam. The man looked after her a moment, then, shaking his head, retreated back toward the stage, where two cast members were whispering.

Hillary motioned for us to continue toward the galley.

As soon as the door between the pantry and dining room closed behind me, I asked, "Jinxed? That sounds a little dramatic."

Hillary laughed off Cassidy's comment. "Just a typical case of preshow jitters. Anything that goes wrong she blames on fate, the stars—"

"Tea leaves?" George suggested.

"Just about," Hillary said. "I doubt she's *seriously* paranoid."

"Who?" Ken asked, looking up from the counter, where he was folding napkins in neat triangles. Quickly he stepped around the counter and relieved Hillary of one of George's parcels.

"Cassidy's convinced someone onboard is out to get her," Hillary said. "That's pretty paranoid, if you ask me."

"Come off it, Hil. I wouldn't call her paranoid. She's got reason to think something funky's been going on around here lately. Especially after what happened," Ken reminded her.

"Like what?" I put the carton of groceries I was carrying on the counter.

"Her locket went missing, for one," Ken said.

"Someone filched it?" George asked.

"Probably. She swears it wasn't very valuable, except to her. But ever since she lost it, she's fallen to pieces on the stage. Something about it being her lucky locket. Cassidy's convinced she can't perform without it."

This didn't bode well for tonight's performance. "Is she the lead?" I asked.

"Yes," Hillary answered. "She plays opposite Toby."

"Who's she?" George looked up from stowing milk cartons in the fridge.

Hillary giggled. "*She* is a *he*. Toby Marchand. That guy with the cute mustache. The Riverside Players are his troupe. Winters, they're based in Minnesota. Summers, they're a traveling summer-stock company. Toby is producer and director, and occasionally he still takes the stage. Tonight he plays the villain."

"Theater people are usually pretty superstitious," I pointed out. "So it makes sense she'd think losing some kind of lucky charm would jinx her."

Ken shook his head. "But that's not all that's gone on. Some of the crew are grumbling too. Even here in the kitchen, stuff's disappearing. Some of the paperwork for the party tonight got lost, including the seating chart."

Hillary rolled her eyes. "Ken, don't make such a big deal of that. So a piece of paper got thrown out—

who cares? We came up with a new chart."

"Why would someone want to fool with a seating plan?" George asked.

"Who knows?" I said, though I was wondering who planned the seating in the first place. Before I had a chance to ask, Ken added, "Okay. But it's a weird coincidence that the cabin assignments got wiped from the computer."

"No big deal there, either," Hillary insisted. "We just reentered the data and made sure our biggest contributors got the best cabins, same as we did first time around."

"It does all seem fairly petty," I said as we started back to retrieve the rest of George's supplies. Ken came with us. When we passed back through the dining room, I noticed only two stagehands were on the stage working on the footlights. Toby and the other actors were gone.

Ken stopped at the top of the gangplank and pointed to the bow of the ship. "Maybe losing, misplacing, or even stealing lists is petty, but one of the lifeboats was unaccounted for last night."

"That's more serious," I commented. My sixth sense—the sense that noticed suspicious activity—was tingling.

George gave me a knowing look.

"But the boat's back now," Hillary said. "I bet

25

someone—or *two* someones—went off for a moonlight row and a swim."

With Ken's help we quickly finished moving Ready, Set, Eat! equipment onto the boat. After I found my cabin assignment, I retrieved my quilted duffle and hoodie from the car and stowed them in my room. Then I set out to find Bess. I found her two decks down, where a member of the engineering crew had directed me to a small room adjacent to the boiler room. As I approached the room I heard raised voices, then a loud crash from just behind the open door.

"Okay, then, show me!" Dylan's voice was mocking.

I couldn't hear Bess's reply. I poked my head inside the doorway. She and Dylan were in front of a large electrical panel. Bess held a small Allen wrench. Dylan stood there, glowering. A large pair of pliers was lying on the floor. I had the distinct impression he'd thrown it there.

A moment later the door labeled BOILER ROOM—KEEP OUT opened. A man limped through, closing the door behind him. He leaned heavily on a wooden cane. In spite of his limp, he had the compact muscular build of an athlete. He was in his fifties now, but when he was young, he must have been really strong. His expression was both annoyed and amused.

His eyes traveled from Dylan, to the pliers on the floor, to Bess—then to the Allen wrench in Bess's hand.

26

"Good. Good. I see you're about to tackle that ornery screw on the electrical-panel door." He addressed Bess, not Dylan. "It's been on my fix-it list for—what would you say, Dylan? About a month now?"

"I just didn't have time to get to it." Dylan's excuse was mumbled, and he shifted his eyes away from the man's piercing blue gaze.

"Right!" The man's tone was tinged with sarcasm. Then he noticed me standing in the opposite doorway. "And you're? . . ."

Bess spoke up. "Cab, this is my good friend Nancy. She's one of the passengers on the cruise tonight." Turning to me, Bess continued, "And this is Cab Mitchell. He's Captain Mike's first mate, and oversees the engineering and maintenance crew on the *Magnolia Belle*."

"Howdy!" he greeted me, poking out his hand. I noticed he had a small anchor tattooed on the back of his left hand. He looked me right in the eye as he spoke, and his face had an open, no-nonsense expression. I decided instantly that I liked him.

"Pleased to meet you," I replied. Then I noticed his cane: It wasn't just sturdy, but an antique as well. Though most of his hand covered the top of the cane, I could see it was intricately carved in the shape of some kind of animal head. I was curious to see what it was. "That's a beautiful cane," I told him, hoping he'd let me examine it. "Is it ebony?"

He arched his eyebrows "You noticed?"

Bess chuckled. "Nancy notices *everything*."

Under Cab's intense stare I felt my cheeks color. "Come off it, Bess," I protested, shooting her a look. I hate having my knack for detecting broadcasted to complete strangers. I turned to Cab. "I was just was curious about the cane. It's so beautiful, and the carving seems unusual. Mrs. Mahoney's late husband, Cornelius, collected animal-head canes. She might be interested in seeing it later."

Cab grinned. "Sure. And I'd be interested in seeing that collection. Never had the means to indulge my own yen to add a couple to my stock. Though for me, a cane is not only a decoration, it's a necessity."

He showed me the top of the cane. "That's amazing!" I said as I looked at the intricately carved animal head. It was a dog—not a ferocious one—just some kind of lapdog, but its expression was fierce, with jaws opened and teeth bared.

"It's beyond amazing, Nancy. You can actually count the teeth," Bess remarked as she examined the carving. "Have you looked at this, Dylan?"

I smiled to myself. Bess's invite to join us was her way of making a peace offering.

"Yeah," he said. "It's pretty cool."

Cab cleared his throat. "Time to get this show on

the road again, wouldn't you say?" he addressed both Dylan and Bess. To me he explained, "I was just about to go over how the steam from the boilers gets to the engine, when we had our little mishap." He cast a glance at Dylan. Dylan pursed his lips, but didn't say anything. Cab turned to me and said, "You're welcome to stay if you're interested."

"Sure." I was curious enough about how the steam engine worked to stay.

Bess bent down to pick up the pliers from behind the door. Dylan grabbed it from her and hung it on a Peg-Board full of tools next to the electrical panel. Bess looked at me from behind his back and shrugged.

Cab opened the door to the boiler room, and a blast of heat rushed out. "Just before Bess and Dylan set out to repair that panel box, Bess was telling me what she knew about steam power."

Dylan looked up at the ceiling and heaved a sigh. "Anyone can find that sort of information."

"True," Bess admitted. "I did look it up online. But seeing the real thing in 3-D—it's so much clearer," she added, forgetting all about Dylan and hurrying over to the two boilers. "These must be the pressure gauges—but where are the safety valves?"

Dylan stood next to me by the door, scratching his head. "How does she know about stuff like safety valves?"

Feeling sorry for the guy, I explained. "Bess is really mechanically inclined. She won a prize in a statewide Mr. Fix-it contest when she was in high-school shop class."

"*Mr.* Fix-it? Uh . . . right!" Now Dylan looked totally baffled. "Why would a girl take shop? I don't get it."

I just shrugged off that last comment and went over to listen to what Cab was telling Bess. They were standing on one side of a boiler and looking at an array of large, sturdy pipes.

Bess tapped the face of one of the gauges. Peering past her shoulder, I saw the gauge had a display of dials and numbers. The upper range of numbers was painted over a red zone marked DANGER.

"What happens if these pressure-release valves fail?" she was asking Cab.

"They don't!" he said abruptly, then patted her shoulder. "Don't worry. These systems are checked out on a regular basis."

I, for one, was relieved to hear that, but Bess looked a little miffed. I could tell she wanted more detailed information. But Cab moved us along to a side room and showed us pipes that fed the fuel to the heaters that sat on top of the boilers. "It's important for the fireman to keep the pressure at around two hundred pounds," he explained.

"Then the steam drives the pistons," Bess said

before he could go on, "which are connected to these rods, that connect to the drive shaft . . ."

Cab whistled softly. "Hey, blondie, you really are something!"

Bess winced at the word *blondie*.

"Those rods are pitman arms," Dylan added, looking relieved he knew something Bess didn't.

Cab wasn't fooled. He gave Dylan a gentle shove. "You're *supposed* to know these things. You've been working on the *Belle* for two months now. And your uncle's been piloting boats like this with you tagging along since you were knee high. This young woman has been onboard for what—five, six hours? I'm impressed."

Bess blushed, but behind Cab and Dylan's backs she gave me a victory sign.

The ship's PA system suddenly crackled to life. "Cab to the wheelhouse. Cab to the wheelhouse." From the drawl, I recognized Captain Mike's voice.

"The master calls!" Cab joked, and turned to Dylan. "I expect you two to finish checking over the circuit breakers. Then keep an eye on that stage crew. They need to rig something for the play that involves the lighting. Don't let them mess up any of our other electrical systems." He started out of the boiler room, then turned and winked at Bess. "And you keep an eye on Dylan. He's trouble!"

4

Mysterious Lights

I adored my cabin. It looked out on the Plantation Deck, on the port side of the ship. As we were sailing upstream, I had a good view of the setting sun, and of the hilly outline of Stony Lonesome Island lying midstream and just north of us.

The breeze blew through the open shutters, and I could hear cheerful splashes of water made as the paddle wheel turned. We'd been under way for less than an hour, but I had already gotten used to the distant chug of the steam engine down in the bowels of the ship.

I dressed for dinner, then checked my reflection in the mirror. My sunscreen had failed me again, and the tip of my nose was sunburned. I tried to mask the redness with some makeup, then, grabbing my small blue purse, hurried down to the Main Deck to meet up with Ned.

Mrs. Mahoney had found him first. They stood against the black wooden railing, watching the sun slowly sink behind the trees on the far shore.

As usual Agnes Mahoney looked terrific. She was wearing a simple, classy pantsuit. Her gray hair blew slightly in the wind, and she looked content and relaxed.

When she saw me coming, she smiled. "Hi, Nancy. Don't you look lovely! I was so glad to hear that Ned would be joining us, though I'm sorry your father has to miss out on this trip."

"It's a mixed bag," I admitted, leaning back against the rail.

That's when I noticed Mrs. Mahoney's necklace. It was ornate, gold, and really gorgeous. The chain was on the long side. A brilliant green gem set in an oval of filigreed gold hung from the center of the chain. "I've never seen that necklace before. It's amazing!"

Mrs. Mahoney fingered it wistfully. "It's a real treasure. It's old as old can be. It belonged to Cornelius's mother, but she used to say that it dates back to the days of Louis the Fourteenth in France!" She held up the gem to the light. "It's the real thing—an emerald."

"And you're wearing it?" Ned visibly gulped.

Mrs. Mahoney looked sheepish. "I shouldn't be. It

is insured, but the fastening isn't as secure as it should be. I keep meaning to bring it to Dave's Jewels and Gems to have him put on a safety chain. But since I seldom wear it, I never get around to fixing it. And I love it—I couldn't resist wearing it on this cruise. It's remarkably lightweight for its size, and works perfectly with my wardrobe for this trip."

"You shouldn't wait on that sort of thing," Ned remarked. "It would be a pity to lose it."

Mrs. Mahoney took a deep breath. "You're right. Even though I'd get the money for it, the piece is irreplaceable—both for sentimental reasons and because it's truly of museum quality." She paused, then seemed to remember something. "Oh, for some reason, museums remind me of Luther. The captain is seating him at our table. What fun that he's sailing along with us!"

Just then a dog yapped. "Whose dog?" Ned wondered out loud.

We all looked toward the barking sound. An athletic-looking woman was heading in our direction. It was Nadine Tucker, the chief benefactor of Animal Haven, one of our local shelters. She had blue eyes, short dark hair, and was carrying a small white dog under one arm. She was also one of Mrs. Mahoney's best friends.

"Nadine!" Mrs. Mahoney cried. "You're back from Hong Kong."

"Last Monday," Ms. Tucker told her, shifting her dog from under her right arm to her left, and air-kissing her friend. The dog was a wiggly bundle and seemed to be dying to be put down so it could explore the ship. "Fizzy Lizzy, would you be quiet!"

"Fizzy Lizzy?" Mrs. Mahoney chuckled. "That doesn't sound like the usual sort of name you give your dogs." Then she remembered, "Nadine, you know Nancy already, and this is Ned Nickerson."

"Son of James Nickerson, of the *Bugle*?"

"The same."

"I ran into your father when I flew in from New York last week. He was on his way to a convention, or else I guess he'd be here."

Mrs. Mahoney tapped Ms. Tucker's arm. "You still haven't explained either the name, or where you got this sweet dog! What is it?"

I recognized the breed instantly. "Bichon frise," I said. When everyone looked startled, I explained, "Once, I worked on a case that required me to go to a dog show. Part of my investigation led me to learn more than I ever wanted to know about dogs."

Ms. Tucker nodded. "I'm not sure Fizz here is a purebred. And, Agnes, she is not mine . . . not *yet,* actually. Animal Haven just rescued her. Her previous owner, Sadie Washington, brought her up from down South after visiting her niece last winter. Fizz was a

35

stray down there. Sadie named her, and then when she passed away last month, her family brought the dog to the shelter. I'm fostering her until we can find her a decent home."

Ned was tickling the dog under her chin. She stopped barking and began licking Ned's hand. "Shouldn't be a problem placing this one. She's pretty affectionate," he said.

"And she's a decent watchdog too—or at least every time she hears a squirrel in the yard, she carries on like a major heist is in progress!" Ms. Tucker said.

"Can she do tricks?" I asked.

"No idea," Ms. Tucker answered. "But she should be able to learn."

"Why?" Mrs. Mahoney inquired.

"Because bichons frises are circus dogs and street performers—that's part of their history, at least," I replied.

"Fascinating," Mrs. Mahoney said, scratching the dog behind her ears. "But not as fascinating as Hong Kong. I want every last detail of your trip! Let's see if we're sitting near each other. And look, here comes the girl with the hors d'oeuvres. Let's try some." Mrs. Mahoney said good-bye to Ned and me, then headed off with her friend.

I watched the two women stroll toward the dining room. A moment later, dressed in her waiter's uniform, Hillary offered them a selection of hors d'oeuvres. After Mrs. Mahoney and Ms. Tucker made their choices, Hillary headed in our direction.

"Hi, guys!" she said. I was grateful that this time she didn't seem particularly interested in Ned.

"These all look great!" Ned said, eyeing the array of minipizzas, tiny quiches, and canapés.

"George's mom has outdone herself again," I said, inhaling the luscious aromas.

As we picked out our treats, Hillary nudged my elbow slightly. "It seems the show will go on," she confided with a knowing smile.

"What happened?" I asked, trying to balance my miniquiche on a tiny napkin.

"Even without her locket, Cassidy Norman got her act together." Hillary paused and grinned at her own pun. "Catch you later," she added, and moved a few feet farther down the deck, offering her tray to some other passengers.

Ned finished munching his pizza, then gestured toward the dining room. Ms. Tucker and Mrs. Mahoney were talking with Ken. "Don't get me wrong," Ned said, "but sometimes I don't understand really rich people. They own such valuable stuff. If I had that necklace, I'd sell it. I'd probably get enough to pay for a dozen kids to spend their whole summer at Camp Muskoka."

"Oh, please!" I protested. "Mrs. Mahoney is one of the most generous people in River Heights. She supports half of the charities in town, with big contributions as well as with her time. You know that!"

Ned looked contrite. "Sorry, Nancy. It's just that seeing her be so careless with something worth so much—"

"She isn't being careless. You know Mrs. Mahoney almost as well as I do. She's careful with everything she owns and she doesn't waste money. She said she's been meaning to bring it into Dave's for ages. She probably didn't have time, what with all the charity work she's been doing lately."

Before I could say more, a spooky *dum-da-dum-dum* chime rang throughout the ship. Ned and I exchanged a glance, then burst out laughing. "The dinner bell?" he asked.

"The dinner bell," I answered.

Ned started toward the dining room.

I hung behind, wanting to savor the breeze a moment longer. I turned back toward the railing. Since I last looked out the window in my cabin, the *Belle* had made good progress toward Stony Lonesome Island. I could actually make out the tall stand of pines perched on the bluff on the island's near shore. We'd probably be reaching it not long after dinner, just as the captain promised.

Over the island the sky glowed a deep indigo, and the last remnants of sunset stained the bluffs a pale pink.

I turned to tell Ned to come and check it out before it all faded. But he was already inside the dining room, talking to one of his father's friends.

Wishing we could share the moment, I gave the island one last look. And blinked.

Was I seeing things?

For a minute I was sure I saw a flashing light rising from the shadows at the foot of the island's bluffs.

I leaned over the railing and squinted. There it was again! A flash of light—a *series* of flashes.

As I stared I realized the flashes had some sort of pattern: three long flashes, a pause, then one long flash, one short, followed by one long.

Morse code! I was sure of it. I wracked my brain, trying to remember the coded alphabet. I'd have to check it out online later.

As I tried to decipher the signal, the sun, already setting, dipped totally behind the horizon. As twilight fell the flashing lights disappeared.

I waited a few minutes longer. But as the sky darkened, all I saw was the last glint of pink brighten the tops of the pines, then quickly fade.

39

5

Blackout!

"**D**id you see that?" Luther's voice made me jump. I turned on my heel. He was standing right behind me, dressed for dinner in a suit and tie.

Still wondering if I hadn't imagined the flashing lights, I said, "Did I see what?"

Luther gave me a puzzled look. "The sunset. It was pretty glorious."

"Yeah, the sunset *was* great. . . ."

"I hear a *but* coming!" Luther must have been talking to Harold Safer, owner of our local cheese shop, a little too much—all he talked about was sunsets! Before I could joke about it, he motioned me toward the dining room. Most of the guests were already inside. I could see Ned with Mrs. Mahoney at a table near the stage. He looked over his shoulder in my direction and waved, and I waved back.

"So what's the *but* about, Nancy?" Luther always takes me seriously.

I took a deep breath. "This sounds crazy, but I thought I saw some kind of signal light. Like Morse code."

Luther stopped in his tracks. "Morse code?" He shook his head. "I watched the whole sunset from right over there." He pointed toward the wheelhouse. "I was with the captain. I didn't see any lights."

"Even just a few moments ago?"

"Even then. Captain Mike and I were looking toward the sunset . . . mainly so we could see Stony Lonesome Island. We were planning tonight's excursion." Luther patted my shoulder. "Sounds like your imagination got the better of you. After all, I just told you the story of the *Lucinda Lu* this afternoon. You were probably remembering that crime was never solved, and what you saw was probably just a trick of light."

I thought a minute as we approached our table. Ned saw us coming and stood up. "Yes, the light was so changeable just then, and the tale of the *Lucinda Lu* was on my mind. I guess I was just seeing things."

Hmm. I'd need to think about it more on my own time.

"Nancy, we've got the best seats in the house," Ned remarked, pulling out my chair.

41

"I'd say so!" Luther enthused as he sat down on one side of Mrs. Mahoney. I was on her other side. Our table was the closest to the stage, but that didn't surprise me. According to Hillary's comments earlier, the biggest contributors scored the best tables, and Mrs. Mahoney was the most generous of all the town's philanthropists. And I knew my dad had given the company a nice tip in advance. Nadine Tucker and some of her friends were seated right behind us. She was finger-feeding bits of bread sticks to her dog. Luther was probably placed at our table as the ship's honorary guest.

Each table had an elaborate floral centerpiece, and every place setting boasted a tiny plastic replica of the *Belle* as a souvenir. Propped against each water glass was the Playbill for that night's performance. I checked out the cast. Besides Cassidy Norman and actor-director Toby Marchand, there were two other men, Grady Morgan and Tom Stein, and one other woman, Angela Como.

Just as the waiters began serving dinner, Captain Mike, dressed in a fresh white uniform, approached the microphone onstage. He introduced himself, then announced that the performance would begin slightly earlier than planned. Pointing to Luther, he said, "We want to button up our theatrics a bit sooner, because tonight we've lucked out. Your River Heights local historian, Luther Eldridge, is on board. Stand up, Luther!"

Shyly Luther rose, and everyone applauded. "Luther here has kindly volunteered to give whoever's interested a moonlight tour of Stony Lonesome Island."

A ripple of excitement ran through the room. The captain made a few more remarks, then joined us for dinner. He sat across from Mrs. Mahoney and entertained us during dinner with tales of his adventures on riverboats.

Dinner was great, but I couldn't wait for the play to start. From what I'd read in the program, the audience got to participate in the play. There were hints for a crime to solve. Finally the waiters finished serving up dessert, tea, and coffee.

The overhead lights flashed three times, then a voice from the back of the dining room announced, "Ladies and Gentlemen, the play is about to begin."

For a moment the whole room went black, except for the safety lights. People gasped. Mrs. Mahoney gripped my arm. A second later the stage lights went up, and the room burst into applause. Except for the glow cast by the wall sconces, the rest of the dining room was almost as dark as a regular theater.

"This is amazing!" Luther whispered, leaning into me and nodding toward the stage.

He was right. The set was a nearly perfect replica of the *Magnolia Belle*'s Star Deck Observation Lounge, except the actors wore late-nineteenth-century costumes. I felt as if I'd be whisked back in a time machine to Mark Twain's America.

Cassidy was already onstage, looking sophisticated, glamorous, and beautiful in her makeup, wig, and gown. She was playing checkers with Toby Marchand. By the second scene of the first act, it became clear that Toby's character was an unscrupulous con man attempting to worm his way into the affections—and fortunes—of a wealthy, lonely widow. Two other characters seemed to have equally shady intentions toward Cassidy: the first mate, and a young woman who was traveling alone. Both were the actors I'd seen onstage earlier that afternoon whispering together during Cassidy and Toby's argument. Grady Morgan played the one good guy—the fictional steamboat's captain.

Midway through the first act I had a pretty good idea of *what* the crime was going to be—certainly nothing short of murder. As the story progressed I sat forward in my seat, eager to garner clues. I knew from Captain Mike's comments that the intermission between the two acts would involve a kind of guess-whodunit game with the audience.

I studied the setup on the stage: All the players were present. Cassidy was still seated across from Toby; the young woman had settled into an easy chair near the game table. The play's captain was over by the map drawer when the first mate walked onto the set and asked "You called, sir?"

As if on cue, all the lights went out—onstage and throughout the dining room—instantaneously followed by a muffled scream. The audience gasped, then began to clap.

I joined in the applause until I noticed that except for red exit safety-lights, the whole ship was plunged into darkness. The wall sconces, the lamps outside on the deck, even the garlands of miniature lights decorating the railings had gone out.

"Why are *all* the lights out?" Captain Mike's bellow pierced the murmurs of the crowd.

"Someone messed up," a male voice cried from the stage.

Nervous chatter began filling the dining room. Chairs shuffled, silverware clattered to the floor, and Fizzy Lizzy began to yap.

I reached into my purse, pulled out my penlight, and turned it on. Everyone at our table looked confused. Ken had pulled a small electric lantern out from behind the bar. He was turning light switches on and off. "Nothing's working. Maybe a fuse blew," he called from across the shadowy room.

The words were barely out of his mouth when all at once the lights flickered, then came back on.

I blinked at the sudden brightness.

A cheer went up from the guests, and the room breathed a collective sigh of relief.

But Captain Mike was not happy. He ran up to the stage and clearly was going to let Toby know it. He smiled at the audience in between whispers to Toby.

The actor lifted his shoulders. "I'm sorry," he said, loud enough for me to hear. "Really. Don't know what happened here. It's never happened before. The lighting crew must have gotten wires crossed."

Some people at another table giggled at Toby's pun.

Captain Mike was still not smiling, but after casting one more scathing glance in Toby's direction, he returned to his seat and sat back down.

Momentarily at a loss for words, Toby took center stage. He cleared his throat, but before he spoke, he looked down at Cassidy.

She was still on the floor of the stage, sitting up. Her bottom lip was trembling, and her expression was beyond furious. A stream of fake blood ran down the back of her dress.

"And how do you explain this?" she challenged Toby.

He reached down to help her up. Ignoring his outstretched hand, she scrambled to her feet. With her laced boot, she kicked aside a big dagger lying on the floor next to where'd she'd fallen. Made of hard rubber, it bounced across the floorboards.

If Cassidy hadn't looked so angry, I would have laughed.

"The lighting crew blew it," Grady said, stepping up to Cassidy's side. "No one did it on purpose."

"You expect me to believe that—after *everything else*?"

I waited for her to launch into her "this ship is cursed" routine, but Toby silenced her with a hard, withering look.

Toby put his hands up and addressed the audience. "It's pretty obvious there was some hitch in the wiring, but I think you all realize that Madame LaMott—Cassidy's character—has just been murdered and *you,* the audience, have to find out whodunit." He paused and added with a wink, "The show, as we say, must go on."

Toby made a grand gesture toward the rest of us. He turned back to his actors and started to tell them to assume the positions they'd be in when the lights would flicker back on in a normal production.

Cassidy continued to pout and stood her ground a moment longer, but after Grady whispered something to her, she got back down on the floor to play dead. She was arranging her gown, and reaching to place the dagger just to the right of her, when Mrs. Mahoney gasped.

"My necklace!" I looked at her neck.

The necklace was gone.

6

Foul Play

whirled around. Mrs. Mahoney was standing, touching her neck. Sure enough, it was bare.

"Maybe it fell off when you got up from the table," Ned suggested. He stooped down to the floor and began searching under the chairs and the table.

"Of—of course!" Relief washed over Mrs. Mahoney's face. She picked up her napkin, then her program, the dessert menu—then she looked under her dessert plate.

Ned crawled out from under the table and dusted off his pants. Looking troubled, he said, "It's not under the table or on the floor around here."

Mrs. Mahoney turned pale. "You—you're positive?"

Ned gave a helpless shrug and caught my eye. From his expression I knew exactly what he was thinking: Agnes Mahoney's heirloom necklace wasn't lost. It was stolen.

"I'll check again," I offered. I flicked my penlight back on, got down on all fours, and inspected the area under the three adjacent tables in between people's legs. I ran my hand along the carpet, feeling for the space between it and the base of the stage. Nothing. I tried to pry up the carpet, in case the necklace had somehow, in the confusion of the blackout, slipped under the rug. But the bound edges of the carpet were taped down.

When I stood up, I chose my words carefully. "When did you first realize you'd lost it?"

Mrs. Mahoney sat down heavily, her eyes welling with tears. But in typical Agnes Mahoney fashion, she pulled herself together. She thought a moment. When she answered me, her eyes were still glistening, but her voice was steady. "Um—just now. When the lights came back on." She stopped and frowned. "No. I didn't *notice* it right then. After the lights went on, I started clapping with everyone else and then . . . Oh, Nancy, I don't remember. I think it was just now, when the actors were about to get back in their positions onstage."

No doubt about it: The necklace hadn't just *fallen* off her neck. Under cover of darkness it was definitely stolen.

With this realization, I wanted to kick myself. When the room went dark and I turned on my penlight, I might have seen whoever had lifted the necklace. But while I swept the stage and the room with the narrow beam of light, I missed my chance.

"Mrs. Mahoney," I said, "I'm afraid there's a thief onboard. There's no other explanation."

"There's got to be. This sort of thing never happens on my watch!" Captain Mike exclaimed. "Besides, how could someone just filch a necklace— in the dark, no less? She lost it somewhere, that's what happened." He sounded incredibly defensive.

"I beg to disagree, Captain Mike." Mrs. Mahoney straightened up in her seat. "I know I had it when I sat down for dinner. I remember fingering it when I was looking at the menu. I had it at least until the lights went out. I'm sure of that. I did jump up when the lights came back on. It could have fallen off then."

"Except if it fell off, we would have found it by now," Luther added.

"The lights weren't out *that* long," Ms. Tucker spoke up. She had come over to our table and had sat down next to Mrs. Mahoney. "Who could have worked that fast?"

"A professional thief," Ned surmised.

"A pretty *wily* thief," Luther added. "Right, Nancy?"

I was only half listening. "Uh, yes." I was scanning the room, trying to see who was present—and who was missing. I realized that all the waiters were accounted for: Ken was still behind the bar; Hillary was holding a pitcher of water near the galley entrance; and two waiters I hadn't been introduced to were standing with white tea towels over their arms, on either side of the doors leading to the deck.

George poked her head out of the kitchen door. She was wearing a white cook's jacket with her jeans. Obviously her mother had needed her for prep work and not for waiting tables this evening. Hillary was whispering something to her. I watched George's expression shift from curious to shocked. She caught my eye. I just nodded at her. I knew she got my message. I'd catch her up on events later.

Looking around the rest of the room, I felt a stab of dismay. There were many suspects aboard, people who could benefit from the money after selling a necklace like Mrs. Mahoney's. Though many people on board were already wealthy, there were a few who were known to be pretty greedy. The necklace could be stashed in just about any pocket or purse. I knew I couldn't ask to search the crowd; aside from insulting most of the River Heights movers and shakers, it would be illegal.

I tried to narrow down the suspects. The most likely people would be closest to our table when the lights went out. Namely, any one of the waiters, any one of the actors—in fact, anybody sitting within a few feet of Mrs. Mahoney. Her necklace had been showy, with a very large emerald. Whoever liked jewels and had sticky fingers could have scoped it out before dinner, when Mrs. Mahoney strolled around the ship, or later, in the dining room.

"I'm still not convinced," Captain Mike said, his frown deepening. He looked up at the stage. "Toby, are you sure you didn't see anything?"

"The lights were out. How could I see?"

"None of us could see," Cassidy spoke up from the stage. She looked as pale as Mrs. Mahoney and was chafing her arms. "I don't understand—if someone stole something, shouldn't we call the police?"

"The police?" Angela Como repeated. The younger actress was sitting on one of the sofas on the set. Her eyes were wide. She looked frightened, and I wondered if she too had valuables on board.

"That's what we'll do. I'll call right now," Captain Mike agreed, though he sounded a bit reluctant. Why? Was he worried about word getting out that his ship wasn't secure? Or was he worried about something else?

I made a mental note to check the *Magnolia Belle's*

history. The captain said nothing like this had happened before, but I was beginning to wonder.

Captain Mike pulled out his cell phone and dialed 911. He explained to the operator what had happened and that he needed to talk directly to the police chief, pronto. She put him through, and after he explained what happened, he listened a moment to someone on the other end, flashed me a questioning look, then handed me the phone.

"Nancy?" I tried not to make a face. It was Chief McGinnis. I should explain that the chief is not my biggest fan. The feeling is mutual. He hates that I tend to solve crimes that stump him; I don't like the way he always tries to take credit for work done by others—not just by me, but by some of the really hardworking officers on his staff.

I took a deep breath before answering. "Yes, Chief McGinnis, it's me."

"Are you sure Agnes Mahoney's necklace was stolen?"

"Looks that way."

I could hear him drumming his fingers on the other end of the phone. He let out a loud, resigned sigh. "Okay. I can't get men out there tonight. Our patrol boat is downriver dealing with a bunch of rowdy kids in a stolen canoe." He hesitated, then asked, "Do you think you could start checking things out there?"

I could hear the reluctance in his voice as he went on. "I'll send the boat up in the morning—unless you think it's an emergency."

"No, that's all right," I told him. "It's nothing we can't handle here. I'll check things out."

"Okay. I told the captain to bring the ship around and head back here, but not to dock until morning. We don't want anyone leaving ship, do we, Nancy?"

"No, sir, we don't," I answered meekly, though I had already planned to tell the captain to make sure no one rowed off on a moonlight excursion tonight.

The chief went on, "I've also asked Captain Mike to give me a crew list over the phone. I'll check them out on the National Crime Fighters Database. Don't mess up any clues, Nancy. And please don't start accusing everyone on board. There are some pretty important people on that boat. . . ."

I only half listened as he went on. Typical Chief McGinnis, he seemed worried that I'd be more of a bother than a help. Even after all the cases he'd seen me handle.

"Not to worry, Chief. I'll be tactful." Well, at least, I'd try.

After I hung up, I handed the phone back to the captain.

He took it and eyed me skeptically. "I'm supposed to believe *you're* a detective?"

"One of the city's best." Mrs. Mahoney leaped to my defense. "Nancy has cracked cases that have had the whole police department stumped."

The captain still didn't look convinced. "You got a license?"

Ned was standing next to me. I could feel him tense, and realized he was about to argue with the captain. I managed to answer first.

"No. I'm just an amateur," I said, and added in my sweetest voice, "but Chief McGinnis put me on the case, so I guess he thinks I can handle it, at least until we get back to town."

Captain Mike shook his head. "Whatever. But if because of you, the crook gets away with this, McGinnis will hear about it from me, the boat's owner, *and* our insurance companies!"

I decided to ignore that. I'd been faced with tough whodunits before, and with patience and enough time, I was nearly always able to crack the case. Captain Mike's doubts and McGinnis's reluctance to let me start the investigation only doubled the fun of the challenge. First, I knew I had to let Captain Mike know who exactly was in charge of this investigation. Gently, of course.

"Captain Mike, do you think that somehow, for the next couple of hours, we could keep people here in the dining room?"

He looked like he was about to argue my point, then slowly nodded. "You mean to keep track of who goes where for a while? Not a bad idea. We'll offer some more coffee and desserts, and maybe I can work something out with Toby for entertainment."

The captain turned to the crowd. "The bad news is we have to head back for River Heights," he began. "And turning the ship around here is a big deal—the navigable channel between Stony Lonesome Island and the bluffs is narrow—that'll make for slow going, even with Cab at the helm." Then, making it seem like an afterthought, he added, "So it would be prudent for everyone to stay right here in the dining area—except for the waitstaff, who can continue to serve you from the bar or galley. There's a thief on this ship, and we don't want any more easy victims," he added.

"What will happen to the fund-raiser?" Ms. Tucker asked. "People have paid for the cruise and the show. Maybe most will understand under the circumstances, but some folks are sure to be upset. If nothing else, it will hurt our future fund-raising efforts—at least the ones hinging on special events."

Toby had come down from the stage. Standing next to the dinner guests, he looked oddly out of place in his nineteenth-century dinner jacket and cravat. But when he spoke, he was all twenty-first-century business. "Mike, there's no reason the play can't go on. Maybe not tonight but tomorrow. We're certainly willing to repeat the whole performance without extra pay."

I watched as the cast members exchanged startled glances. But none of them objected openly to the director's impromptu offer.

For the first time in the last half hour, Captain Mike smiled. He pounced on Toby's offer. "It's a deal!"

"And maybe by morning we'll have found the necklace," Ms. Tucker added. "I, for one, can't believe someone had the gall to steal it with all these people—potential witnesses—watching."

7

Muffled Voices

Mike asked Toby to organize some entertainment for the next hour or so.

When we left the dining room together, I knew people were wondering why *I* got to leave the room, but Captain Mike had actually decided on his own that it was best that *everyone* on board didn't know I was working the case. Good thinking.

"What gets me," I said as we walked onto the deck, "is how someone could have rigged all the lights on the ship to fade out with the lights onstage."

"Maybe one of Toby's lighting crew is in cahoots with the thief," he suggested. "I can't quite believe it's any kind of coincidence, but have you seen Dylan in action yet?"

At first I thought he was changing the subject;

then I remembered Dylan down by the electrical panels that afternoon, ready to loosen a delicate nut with a pair of humongous heavy-duty pliers. I tried to be tactful. "Um, yes, I have."

My tact fell on deaf ears. "He's a complete klutz. Maybe he did something with the circuit breakers. He's stationed down there with your friend for the evening shift."

"Still, Dylan messing up would be a crazy coincidence," I reminded him.

"True, but I'd check it out if I were you. If you need help figuring out the wiring or anything, if your friend can't help you, Cab or one of the other engineers can. Meanwhile I've got to give the crew list to the cops."

We parted company on the deck. Captain Mike headed up to the wheelhouse, and I went down the two flights of stairs to the engineering department. Bess was sitting on a table, her legs dangling, her attention fixed on some kind of manual. Dylan was pacing the floor in front of her. She seemed totally oblivious to his presence.

As I walked in, he stopped pacing and faced me. "Would you believe it? This girl thinks *I* had something to do with the ship's lights going out."

"Well, you could have!" Bess declared, then seemed to realize Dylan was talking to me. "Nan, what are you doing down here? I managed to flip the lights back on, and—"

"Flip the lights back on?" I hurried over to the electrical panel. Indeed, all the black circuit breakers were in the ON position. "You mean it was just a circuit breaker disabled?"

Bess scoffed. "Of course not. *Somehow*"—she gave Dylan a long, meaningful look—"the main switch had been turned off. Luckily the backup generators kicked in, so the engine didn't lose power, and the safety lights in here stayed on. When I got back here, I figured—"

"When you got back here from where?" I asked Bess.

Dylan folded his arms across his chest and looked with great satisfaction at Bess. "Nice to hear someone else getting grilled."

"Grilled? Nancy's just asking me a ques—" Bess cut herself off. "Nancy, you have that look in your eyes. Why all the questions? What's happening?"

"You don't know?" No sooner had the words passed my lips than I realized neither she nor Dylan had been in the dining room. I leaned one hip on the desk next to Bess and told her. "Mrs. Mahoney's emerald necklace was stolen."

Bess's eyes grew big. Dylan whistled softly. "How?" he asked.

"You don't look surprised," I commented.

Dylan shrugged. "Just one more crazy incident since this boat left New Orleans last month."

"What incidents?" Bess looked at him. "You didn't tell me the cruise is jinxed."

I was surprised to hear her use the word. "What makes you say jinxed?"

Bess blushed. "Well—I overheard someone—I never did see who, but it was a *guy,* of course." She stopped and gave Dylan a pointed look. "He said women shouldn't be on the crew of this boat—even *temporary* crew. Women on board jinx all ships. 'Every sailor *knows* that.' That's what he said."

"Hey, don't blame me. I never said that." Dylan looked hurt. "I like having girls on the ship."

I was sure he did. If nothing else, this guy was a flirt. It's just that he probably hadn't encountered anyone remotely like Bess before. His usual come-on wasn't working.

"Even if it was jinxed," Dylan added, "it's not your fault. Stuff's been happening since long before you came on board."

"Like what?" Bess asked, and I repeated what I'd heard from Ken and Hillary.

"It's not jinxed, Bess," I told her, and filled her in on the rest of that night's events. In the process I had to let Dylan know I was investigating the case.

Bess sighed when I'd finished. "Knowing the way you work, Nancy, everyone's still a suspect. I mean, you haven't narrowed things down yet." Her voice held a question.

Before I could answer, Dylan broke in. "You can narrow things down real fast right here, starting with both of us. We're in the clear."

I knew Bess couldn't be involved and was pretty sure Dylan didn't have the know-how to help pull off some jewelry caper, but I couldn't resist asking. "And what makes you say that?"

I give him credit. He didn't squirm. He just answered bluntly, "We weren't out here. We were both in the ship's workshop when the lights went out."

"As soon as they did, I started rummaging for a flashlight, then the generator kicked in a second later," Bess added.

"Where's the shop?" I asked. Cab hadn't included it in the earlier tour.

"Back here," Bess said. She led the way across the boiler room. One of the crewmen was bent over a pipe leading from the fuel tank to the nearest boiler. He'd taken off his shirt, and his skin glistened with sweat. He looked up as we passed, and smiled.

I smiled back, but made a note to find out his name and to question him later.

"Here's the shop," Bess said, opening the door. Entering the room, I inhaled an odd mixture of odors: the pungent smell of fuel combined with the clean scent of sawdust. The lights were still on, and Bess's old pink "work" sweater was still neatly draped over a workbench. "We were sanding down these chairs that are scheduled for painting tomorrow."

"Did you have the door open?"

The two exchanged a glance. "Yes," Bess said.

"No," Dylan contradicted.

Bess shot me an apologetic look. "I'm not really sure."

"Whatever," I said, masking my disappointment. I should know by now. People in general aren't very observant. "But did you hear anything before or after the lights going out? And was that guy around?"

"You mean Nelson?" Dylan said. "No. He turned up just a few minutes ago, to check something with the fuel lines. Beats me what or why."

"Because there might have been some sort of momentary glitch between the outage and the generator taking over," Bess pointed out.

Dylan rolled his eyes.

Before they could get into another argument, I said, "Okay, so Nelson wasn't here, but did you hear anyone else?"

Both of them shook their heads. Then Dylan's face

screwed up in a frown. "Wait a minute . . . I might have. I heard some weird tapping or thumping noise—"

"Tapping?" Bess broke in and shot Dylan a withering look. "What you heard was the boiler, Dylan. You know, like, heat pipes banging in the walls . . ."

"It wasn't banging," he insisted. "It was more of a thump thump thump."

"A thump isn't a tap!" Bess insisted.

"Whatever, I heard it."

"You're hearing things." Bess refused to concede her point.

The two were now facing each other.

"I know what I heard!" Dylan's voice rose.

"As if you know the difference between a tap and a thump," Bess countered.

I mumbled good-bye, then marched out. I wasn't up for another round of Bess vs. Dylan.

Whatever Dylan heard, or thought he heard, didn't seem very helpful. The little I knew of Dylan and the amazing amount I knew about Bess all pointed toward her being right. Dylan's noise came from the boiler, not from some person lurking around the boiler room or electrical panels.

Between all that heat and those bad smells, I decided I needed some air. I avoided the dining room, and after checking that the *Belle*'s two lifeboats were still accounted for, I strolled toward the stern and leaned back against the starboard railing. The full moon was up, half of it already visible over the high bluffs of the right-hand shore. From what I could see, the boat was just starting to swing around. As Captain Mike had warned, turning around in the narrow channel would be slow going. But probably better than sailing an hour north of Stony Lonesome Island, where the river ran deeper.

After drawing a few deep breaths of fresh air, my head cleared, and gradually I began to cool down in the evening breeze.

My visit belowdecks had proven profitable on one score: Whoever had taken the necklace definitely had an accomplice who knew the exact moment in the play to flip the main switch on the electrical panel.

Had it been a set, prearranged time? I doubted it, because the play could have started a few minutes earlier or later on any given night—and tonight it had started early.

Which meant the thief and the helper had some way of signaling each other. But how?

I was pondering that thought, when suddenly I heard a muffled voice.

It came from somewhere below me. I turned and leaned out over the railing, and tried to listen.

The splash of the paddle wheel made it hard to hear.

All at once, out of the corner of my eye, I thought I saw something move farther down the deck, toward the bow of the ship. I turned and looked. There was a figure leaning over the railing, half hidden in the shadows of the wooden columns that supported the deck above. Again I heard voices—definitely more than one.

I peered over the railing a second time. A small boat was drifting alongside the *Magnolia Belle*. It was painted a dark color that reflected no light. It seemed to huddle in the large shadow cast by the *Belle* in the moonlight.

The craft's maritime lights, if it had them, were not lit, and the vessel bobbed eerily in the water like some kind of phantom ship.

8

A First Suspect

Who's there?" **The gruff** voice made me jump. It came from the shadowy figure near the *Belle*'s bow. At first I thought it was addressing the people in the small boat. Then I realized its profile had shifted: It was looking at me. I saw it was a man, and as he stepped out of the shadows and began limping toward me, I recognized him.

"Cab?"

"What are *you* doing here?" he asked.

"Came out for some air—but what's going on?" I pointed down at the small craft. I noticed then that Cab was holding a flashlight.

"Just a couple of night fishermen. Saw us starting to turn around in these narrows here and worried we were in trouble."

Propping himself against the railing, he leaned over, then cupped his hands over his mouth and shouted to the occupants of the boat below. "Like I told you, we'll be all right."

A voice called back. "Just checking up on you guys." The voice had an accent I couldn't place—maybe eastern European.

"We're fine. We've got a bit of a problem on board and are heading back toward River Heights. Everything's okeydokey!"

"Okeydokey?" I repeated. The only person I'd ever met who used that term was Hannah. She was full of quaint old-fashioned expressions that made me laugh, and sometimes drove my friends crazy. But *okeydokey* really wasn't appropriate, considering what was going on on our ship.

Cab waved his flashlight at the boat. It kicked up its motor and chugged off toward the eastern shore of the river, heading for Martin's Cove at the foot of the bluffs—one of the Muskoka's prime spots for night angling.

As soon as the boat departed, Cab turned to me. "Didn't want those dudes to know what was happening on board. Wasn't even sure they were from around here."

"I wouldn't know," I admitted. Then I remembered something the captain said. "I thought you'd be piloting the ship for this stretch of river."

Cab shrugged. "Plans changed. Captain Mike told me what happened during the play. A shame, that's what it is, a real shame. These nice folks come and pay big bucks to support local charities, and then *poof*!" He snapped his fingers together. "They get ripped off. Anyway, after the captain called the police, he took over the wheel. We saw this boat pull up, and I thought I'd better check it out. Never know; maybe the people on board were in league with the crooks." He paused, then gave me a hearty pat on the shoulder.

"But I don't have to tell you that, do I, Nancy Drew? I hear the police chief himself thinks you're a pretty sharp detective. Not that I'm surprised," he added. "It's clear you've got a sharp eye, like your pal Blondie said earlier."

He had started back toward the wheelhouse, and I decided to go with him. As we walked, he continued to talk. "We usually wouldn't make a U-turn until MacPhee's Landing, where the charts say the river runs broad and deep."

"Yeah, the captain told me that, and it makes sense. Meanwhile I tried to check out who threw the main light switch downstairs on the electrical panel."

"Someone threw the main switch?" Cab looked shocked. Then he frowned. "You sure it wasn't one of Dylan's snafus?"

"He wasn't anywhere near the panels when it happened."

"So someone else is involved. Whoever stole the necklace is working with someone who's savvy about a ship's electrical systems." He lifted two fingers. "Two thieves."

As we reached the wheelhouse, Luther ambled in. "Hope you don't mind that I left the dining room, but I wanted to check up on our planned excursion to the island."

"What excursion?" Cab asked.

"To Stony Lonesome Island. That's why the captain brought me along," Luther said. "I'm supposed to lead a little side trip to the island and relate some of its history."

"That's the first I've heard of it!" Cab sounded annoyed. He looked at the captain. "You should have cleared that with me."

The captain's eyebrows shot up. "It's not your call, Cab. This is my gig, remember?"

"Right, I'm just the first mate."

I thought I detected a note of sarcasm in Cab's voice. Suddenly I wondered if these two men had some kind of past history.

"Whatever your plan was, you have to call it off," Cab declared.

Captain Mike looked like he was about to argue

the point. Cab didn't give him a chance. "Your ship is the scene of a crime. Whoever snatched that bracelet, pin, or whatever it was, is still on board—unless they already made off in one of those lifeboats."

"They didn't," I said. "I checked them out already."

"I'm not calling off the plan. I'm just delaying it." The captain spoke right past Cab's shoulder, directly to Luther. "We'll make it a day trip, tomorrow, once we've solved this little mystery. But at the moment, as Nancy suggested earlier this evening, no one is going to leave the ship."

Luther looked crestfallen. "I understand," he said. "I'll go back down to the dining room and tell the folks interested in the side trip that maybe tomorrow we'll get to it."

After Luther left, I asked the captain if there was some way to know what workers had come on board the ship while we were docked in River Heights. I was beginning to think that stealing Mrs. Mahoney's necklace wasn't such a random act. Had someone actually cased the passengers? Did the culprit have a contact in River Heights?

He told me they kept a logbook of all workers and delivery personnel that came on board whenever they docked in any given town. While Cab went to retrieve it from the office, just off the pilot's room, the captain asked me if I had seen Ned.

71

"He's still in the dining room, I guess," I told him as I stared out the window. We had successfully turned around, and the *Belle* was slowly making its way back downstream.

"Good. I'll catch up with him there."

Cab returned with the logbook before I could ask the captain why he needed to talk with Ned. I checked over the day's entries. Only three workers came on board; besides George and her mother for Ready, Set, Eat!, there was only Melissa Wong from Petal Wings, the ritziest florist in River Heights.

George and her mother were definitely in the clear. Aside from the fact that I knew them both so well and could vouch for their honesty, they hadn't been in the dining room during the blackout. As for Melissa—she was such a workaholic and so busy building her business, I couldn't even imagine her having time to hatch robbery plots.

I couldn't completely rule her out, as she certainly had access through her business to most of the wealthy households in town. But when it came to clothing and jewelry, Melissa wouldn't know the difference between an emerald and a diamond. She was oblivious to everything but flowers, flower, flowers.

Thinking of Melissa's elaborate flower arrangements on each of the dining-room tables, I was suddenly inspired. All those leaves, flowers, ferns, and mosses would make the perfect hiding place for stolen jewels. Later on that night I would go back to the dining room and check out my hunch.

As I scoured the logbook for evidence, Cab and the captain were poring over a map. I had just closed the book when I spotted George. She had taken off her white uniform jacket and was wearing a red cotton camisole that skimmed the top of her jeans. She was waving at me through the glass window of the wheelhouse. Then she mouthed the words. "We need to talk, now!" She started to hurry away from the window.

I replaced the book, and left to find George.

She was standing right next to the wheelhouse and looked as if something terrible had happened. "Nancy, we've got to talk!" Her tone was urgent.

"What's up?"

"Not here!" she whispered, and pulled me aside. "Downstairs. The kitchen's quiet now. Everyone's in the dining room. They've got this wild karaoke thing going on. Hurry. There's no time to waste!"

We both hurried down the side stairs, then slipped through the back of the dining area into the pantry. Only the under-the-counter lights were lit. George poked her head into the kitchen. I noticed it was already cleaned up: The stainless-steel counters and appliances glowed in the low light.

"Good, no one is around." She stopped for a moment, then blurted out. "Nancy—don't take this the wrong way, but . . . they think Ned did it."

"Did what?" I asked.

"Stole Mrs. Mahoney's necklace."

My jaw felt like it dropped down to my feet. Then I decided this was one of George's less successful jokes. *"Right!"* I laughed in her face.

"I'm serious. You don't think I'd make up something like that, do you?"

She had me there. "Well, no, but . . . George, who are *they*?"

"Hillary, and the captain, and the first mate."

"Hillary, as in Hillary the *waitress*?" I couldn't quite wrap my mind about the idea that anyone would even remotely connect Ned with a theft.

"Yeah, that Hillary." George didn't sound like Hillary's biggest fan. "She says she overheard Ned talking about how much Agnes's necklace was worth."

"What in the world gave her—," I started to protest. Then I remembered my conversation with Ned before dinner on the deck. Hillary had been hovering in the vicinity, handing out hors d'oeuvres. She had overheard us and jumped to all sorts of crazy conclusions. I started to smile. "Oh, I can clear that up."

"Don't be so sure," George warned glumly. "Don't forget, Ned was right there at your table when the theft occurred—and Hillary told the captain he was crawling around under the table, *pretending* to look for it afterward."

Suddenly replaying the whole scene in my head, I realized how bad this must look for Ned. "Oh, man!" I cried. "This is crazy. You know he wouldn't steal a flea from a dog's back."

"Of course, I know that—so do you," George said. "But I thought you might want to warn him, especially since it gets worse: Captain Mike called the police and asked for a background check on Ned!"

I winced. Ned hasn't been one of Chief McGinnis's favorite people ever since Ned's dad wrote a scathing *Bugle* editorial about lax police practices.

George gave me a quick, supportive hug. "Of course they won't find anything. Still, you should warn Ned."

I intended to, and yet a part of me wondered if I was playing fair. My own personal rule when I was on a case was never to rule out *anyone* until I could actually clear them with interviews and enough clues pointing to another suspect. But at that moment, Ned was the top suspect, any way you sliced it.

9

A Vicious Turn

The lights in the dining room were dimmed. Tall, burly Jack Halloran was standing stage center, holding a microphone, in the midst of a karaoke rendition of an early Beatles song. The clean-cut CEO of Rackham Industries cut a totally ridiculous figure, gyrating to the slow rhythm, and the room was in stitches.

Ned was no exception. Seated back at our table, only a foot from the stage, he was doubled over with laughter. On his left, Luther was chuckling. On his right, Mrs. Mahoney was smiling, though as I watched, her hand traveled to her neck, and I realized that inwardly she was still extremely upset about losing the heirloom.

Mr. Halloran finished his stint, and the room broke into raucous applause. Before the next act went on, I walked up to our table, dreading the moment when I'd have to burst Ned's happy bubble. That, however, would have to wait until later, when I could catch him alone. Besides, George had offered to come with me to talk to him. I decided to take her up on that, but I wanted to be sure I had the captain in tow. I wanted him to be present to see firsthand that Ned was innocent and did not have the necklace in his possession. The very idea that Hillary had accused him made me mad.

"Hey," I said as I approached. Ned pulled up an empty chair from Ms. Tucker's table. I wondered where she was.

People had gotten up and were now milling around the bar, or table hopping.

"Any luck?" Ned asked under cover of the chatter of the room.

I didn't know how to answer. I couldn't lie, especially to Ned. "No definite leads."

Toby Marchand took the mike, saving me from having to elaborate further about the investigation. "Ladies and gents, as Jack Halloran just demonstrated, there's a wealth of untapped talent in your good city—even if some of it is going to the dogs." Groans and laughter rippled through the audience. Toby silenced the crowd by raising his hand. "So now let me introduce our next act: Ms. Nadine Tucker and her canine wonder, Fizzy Lizzy!"

77

"Dog tricks?" Luther looked at me.

"Guess so," I said.

"Nadine's usually such a behind-the-scenes sort of person," Mrs. Mahoney remarked, puzzled. "What in the world possessed her to take to the stage with that dog?"

"Maybe she's just doing her bit," I suggested. "She's trying to help salvage the fund-raiser and give everyone a good time."

Still holding the dog, Ms. Tucker motioned for Grady to join them on the stage. He had unearthed a red plastic hula hoop from the company's stash of props. Positioning himself across the stage from Ms. Tucker, he held up the hoop. Fizzy Lizzy began to wiggle and yap, and looked expectantly at the hoop.

With a rather self-conscious flourish of her hand, Ms. Tucker put the little dog down. Instantly she bolted upright, her short fluffy tail thumping the floorboards. Grady held up the hoop with one hand and snapped his fingers. Fizzy Lizzy raced across the stage and leaped through the hoop.

We all cheered. Then without further prompting, the little dog stood up on her hind legs and hopped a few steps closer to stage center, where she hopped around in a circle, before dropping down again on all fours. She then ran back to Ms. Tucker, who fed her a dog treat.

"Bravo, Fizzy!" Mrs. Mahoney led the cheers as

Ms. Tucker scooped up the dog and tucked her under her arm. She beamed like a proud mother.

"That's no ordinary dog," Ned remarked, jumping up with the rest of the room and giving the animal a standing ovation.

"It's pretty well trained," I remarked. I was also on my feet, clapping so hard my hands hurt. I was applauding Ms. Tucker as much as Fizzy Lizzy. It took nerve to go onstage, even in front of a friendly audience. My recent brush with acting, even just in front of a film crew, made me more than sympathetic to stage fright.

"Who trained that dog, anyway?" Luther asked over the noise of the applause.

I was wondering the same thing, when Cab came up to our table. He leaned over, and under cover of the loud applause, he whispered, "Nancy, the captain needs to see you now—and could you please ask Ned to come with you."

My heart froze in my chest. But before I could react, I heard Fizzy Lizzy's happy yapping switch to a growl, and then to a series of loud barks.

"Fizzy, calm down!" Ms. Tucker cried as I glanced back up at the stage.

Fizzy had no intention of calming down. She squirmed and growled, then jumped out of Ms. Tucker's arms. Growling and barking, she raced toward the footlights. "Come back here!" Ms. Tucker cried.

Fizzy wasn't listening. Still growling, she leaped over the footlights and practically did a somersault before landing hard on all fours. She aimed herself in the direction of our table—actually, directly toward me. I put my arms up and started to swerve away from her open mouth. But she barreled right past me and locked her jaws on Cab's left leg.

"AHHHHHHH!" he yelled in pain.

Ned grabbed Fizzy's collar and yanked the dog off Cab. Grabbing the edge of the table with one hand, he lifted his cane with the other and brandished it over the dog. At the sight of the cane, the dog cowered back into Ned's arms and began to whimper.

Cab roared, "Delta . . . you little creep!"

Delta? That was odd. But so was everything else about this incident.

As he began to swing the cane down, I reached up and grabbed it from behind. It took all my strength to yank it away from the furious first mate.

"Cab, stop it! The dog was just upset by something," I cried. I looked over at Ned. The dog was shivering and curled against him.

Ms. Tucker had climbed down off the stage. She stooped down over Fizzy. "What happened?" she addressed the dog in a soothing tone. She held out her hand. Fizzy sniffed it, then licked it.

Mrs. Mahoney grabbed Ms. Tucker's tote as Ned

handed the dog back to Ms. Tucker. Continuing to use soothing terms, Ms. Tucker deposited the animal back in the carry bag. She zipped it up securely and put the bag on a chair seat, facing away from Cab.

"I'm so sorry!" she apologized to Cab. "I've never seen her act this way."

Cab's face was red with rage, and I could see a pulse beating in his neck. He was, rightly, still agitated, but he visibly struggled to master his emotions. His voice was tight as he addressed Ms. Tucker. "Just keep that animal away from me . . . and I'd watch her around other passengers. She's got a vicious streak."

He started to walk away, when I noticed the leg of his pants. A red stain was spreading over his white fabric. "Cab, you're hurt! She really bit you. She broke through your skin."

"I'll be all right," he mumbled, and tried to keep walking, leaning heavily on his cane.

"Let me look at that!" Dr. Berson said. Dr. Berson, a good friend of my dad's, and our family doctor, had hurried up to our table. He put a restraining hand on Cab's shoulder. "At the very least we have to disinfect that wound. Have you had a tetanus shot recently?"

"Yeah, yeah . . . and I'm all right, I tell you," Cab protested.

"Cut the tough-guy act," Dr. Berson said in a no-nonsense tone I knew all too well. Cab had no choice but to let the doctor tend to him. "Let me look at that, and would someone get me a first-aid kit?" Ken passed a red and white first-aid box over from behind the bar. I took it and brought it to Dr. Berson.

When I handed it to him, I noticed the doctor had rolled up Cab's pant leg. The bite was on the back of his calf. As he wiped away the blood with an antiseptic cloth, I could see the bite was not deep. Close to the wound was a tattoo. Above a colorful ruffled collar was the grotesquely grinning face of a clown.

Cab and the doctor headed up to the wheelhouse to find the captain and get permission to open the ship's emergency store of medicine and antibiotics.

A moment later Captain Mike's voice came over the PA. At the time I didn't register the significance of his announcement. He said guests were now free to roam the rest of the ship. They could retire to their cabins or come up to the Star Deck Observation Lounge for after-dinner drinks.

Though the side trip to Stony Lonesome Island was postponed, he was sure Luther Eldridge would enjoy regaling everyone with tales of the island and some local history.

When the captain finished, Ned turned to me. "Let's go hear Luther. I've always wanted to get the real scoop about that island!"

"Me too," I admitted, "but I'll have to put it off a bit. I need to talk to the actors first." We agreed to meet up later, when I knew I could no longer put off questioning the one suspect I was sure was perfectly innocent.

Toby had gathered his players and crew on the stage to plan the next day's performance. I waited until he finished discussing the rehearsal schedule before I spoke up.

"If you guys don't mind, I'd like you all to hang around here a few minutes longer. The captain would like me to question each of you about the missing necklace."

"You don't think one of us took it?" one of the stagehands asked.

"Right now, *anyone* could have taken that necklace. It's my job to narrow things down, and any of the actors onstage at the time—or any of the crew in the wings—might have witnessed something that can help us find the thief." I turned to Toby and gave him a look to indicate that I hoped he'd support me.

Toby's response was perfect. "Anything we can do to help, Nancy."

I questioned the lighting crew first. None of them had seen anything unusual during the blackout or, when I pressed them, just before.

I learned that the staged blackout was affected by a

switch rigged up to the main lighting panel and situated in the wings. Earlier that day they had tied in the lines for the dining room's overhead lights to that switch. Two of the crew had gone down to the ship's main electrical box with their walkie-talkies, just to temporarily turn off circuit breakers and cut the juice to the dining room during the rewiring process going on upstairs.

I jotted this down in the little notebook I always carry with me, then told the crew they could leave.

When they cleared the room, only Toby, Grady, Angela, Tom, and Cassidy remained. "First of all, did anyone here see anything unusual? Actually," I said, "you're all actors with good memories. Can anyone tell me who they noticed around that front table just before the robbery? If you don't know the names, that's okay; just a description of the people would help."

Grady scrunched up his face, then shook his head. "Only the waiter—or a couple of waiters. One was pouring coffee right before the blackout, and the other, the pretty girl . . ."

"Hillary," Toby said.

"Anything else, Grady?" I encouraged him to go on.

"Nope."

I got more or less the same response from everyone onstage. Waiters were milling around the tables. Ken was behind the bar. I was just feeling like I'd

84

reached another dead end when Toby spoke up.

"Personally, I think someone had cased Mrs. Mahoney's jewelry collection prior to the theft."

"Toby!" Cassidy exclaimed. "You're always trying to complicate things."

I ignored her comment. Toby had a point. "What makes you say that?"

Toby winked at me. "You forget. I'm a playwright, and my plays are mainly mysteries. It's too much of a coincidence that Mrs. Mahoney and her necklace were the mark. Someone knew who she was, and what she'd be wearing."

Toby was only partly right. Mrs. Mahoney never wore that necklace, so no one would know ahead of time she owned it. Still, her jewelry was worth plenty. "So then, I suppose my next question should be: Does anyone here know Mrs. Mahoney, or anyone for that matter, in River Heights?"

No one answered, but Angela shifted uncomfortably in her seat. I looked her in the eye, and her gaze shifted. "Angela, you know someone in town here?"

Angela nodded. Her eyes welled up. "Umm—not exactly, but I have a cousin who lives a few miles north of town. Her name's Melissa Russo. Maybe you know her?"

I didn't.

"I doubt she knows Mrs. Mahoney," Angela said,

wringing a tissue in her hand. "I guess you have to check. But she wouldn't steal anything . . . ever."

"Oh, Angela, you're such a fool," Cassidy said with evident disgust. "Of course she didn't steal anything. She wasn't even on board the ship. This is all such a waste of time."

"As opposed to the fuss you made about your locket?" Grady spoke up.

Cassidy shot him a withering look, then slumped down in her chair and tapped her foot impatiently.

I tried to ignore Cassidy's outburst, but why in the world did Angela look so nervous? It seemed unlikely her cousin would move in Mrs. Mahoney's circles. Still, you never know. I asked for Melissa's number just in case and jotted it down.

I told everyone they were free to leave. Toby, however, came up to me. "I didn't mean to point a finger at Angela."

I shrugged off his comment. "I doubt her cousin is involved in this. Still, I'll have to check it out. And thanks for the suggestion. It makes sense that someone connected with the theft might have contacts scouting potential marks first."

"Ah, we writers have to know how criminal minds work. . . ."

"Only when it's convenient," Cassidy said as she passed by.

10

Betrayed

I was still pondering Cassidy's remark half an hour later. What was her motive to direct my suspicions toward Toby? I couldn't fathom why. Then I remembered her locket. It was still missing, and it had gone missing before tonight's guests had come on board.

Which, by default, ruled out any of the guests as being responsible for that missing piece—and likely, Mrs. Mahoney's missing piece. "Yes!" I stopped midway on the deck leading to the stairs and pumped my fist in the air. That should also rule out Ned. The captain and Chief McGinnis can't deny that reasoning.

I started up toward the Star Deck. Halfway up the steps I ran into the captain. He was *not* the picture of happiness.

"Where have you been?"

I resented his tone, but tried to keep my cool. "Questioning the players."

"That was a waste of time. I told you to come to the wheelhouse right away. We've already got a pretty strong suspect—but maybe you knew all about this already?"

"I did—and Ned didn't do it. I can rule him out."

"How convenient."

He didn't have to sound so snide about it. We had reached the top of the steps. I stopped and told him, "Listen, you have to trust me. . . ."

The captain rolled his eyes. "I wasn't born yesterday—he's your boyfriend."

"I've had to be objective about people close to me before. But this time, the evidence points to someone *other* than Ned."

"Why?"

"Because whoever stole Mrs. Mahoney's emerald was on this ship before it ever reached River Heights."

"And the evidence?"

"Cassidy Norman's missing locket. It disappeared before you got to River Heights." I tried not to sound too smug.

For a moment Captain Mike almost looked convinced. Then a slow, catlike smile spread across his face. "Cute. But Chief McGinnis's girl detective forgot something—the possibility the two robberies are not connected."

I just stared at him, and though it killed me to admit it out loud, I said, "I hadn't thought of that."

We went together to Ned's cabin. He opened the door. At the sight of the captain, his smile faded. "Uh, hi, Captain Mike." He tried to catch my eye. I avoided meeting his gaze as we entered the room. Ned was in the midst of unpacking his things.

"Who's doing the honors here?" Captain Mike looked at me.

I took a deep breath and told Ned outright that he was a suspect.

"You're putting me on!" He looked from me to the captain, then back again, and his expression darkened. "Nancy, don't tell me you believe this."

"Of course I don't," I blurted out, "but there's some evidence, and we've just got to prove you don't have the necklace."

Ned turned away from me. I could tell he wasn't just hurt, but really angry. I have to give him credit, though—when he faced the captain, he sounded fairly calm. "Okay. Search me. Search this entire room."

The captain made Ned turn out his pockets, and he lifted Ned's mattress to inspect underneath. He riffled through all his drawers, the narrow closet, his shaving kit, and finally, his suitcase. "Okay, so far so good," Captain Mike finally declared.

"Glad you think so," Ned responded, barely masking his growing annoyance. "But what beats me is what made anyone suspect me in the first place. The dining room was full of potential suspects."

I'll give it to Captain Mike. He's a gruff guy, with questionable manners, but after not finding the jewelry, he seemed to soften slightly toward Ned. He laid out the evidence. As he spoke, I watched Ned's shoulders relax.

"That whole thing's a big misunderstanding."

"Nancy already told me that. But I still had to check you out. Sorry," the captain said. "I'm tempted to believe you, and I'll notify Chief McGinnis immediately that you seem to be in the clear. Still, until we find the necklace and actual culprit—"

Ned put a hand up to stop him. "I know the drill. I've been around Nancy long enough to understand that I'm still a potential suspect, but just farther down your list."

Captain Mike headed back to the wheelhouse and his office, and I was left with Ned. There was a moment's awkward silence.

"I . . . ," we both blurted out together, and then Ned gave a nervous laugh. "You first," he said.

"I'm sorry, Ned. I never suspected you for an

instant, you know that—but Captain Mike had called McGinnis, and I couldn't just drop it. . . ."

Ned shrugged. "Yeah, well, it still stings, Nancy, but I understand. So let's just drop it." He squeezed my hand, but neither of us were ready for an apologetic kiss. After a moment, he asked lightly, "So who else is on the list?"

"No one, yet. But I got Tonya Ward to fax me some of the information Chief McGinnis dug up about the crew. I want to see if George can check out some of the players and the crew on the Internet."

"Nice work!" Ned said, giving my shoulders a squeeze. "Always helpful to have a friend in the chief's receptionist, eh?"

We headed off to George's cabin. She was quartered down with the rest of the crew. Because the ship sailed with a pared-down staff for these quick overnight bookings, she had merited her own cabin, right next door to her mother's.

I can't say I was surprised to find George sitting cross-legged on the lower bunk, staring at the screen of her laptop. She greeted us with a distracted wave of her hand. "I'm checking out crew info. Pretty interesting stuff." I should add I was also not surprised she'd beaten me to the punch on getting information.

When I'm on a case, I tend to want to see people

face-to-face first—to interview them, to read their body language. As any one of my friends would tell you, I'm above all a people person. George likes people too, but she will turn to a computer first to solve problems.

"What kind of stuff are you looking for?" Ned asked, dragging up a chair and trying to check out the laptop's screen.

"Background information on the crew. I plugged in all the names I was able to download from the company's employee database."

I gulped. "You mean you got into the personnel files of this ship's owner?"

"Not to worry. Their security was so lax they were asking for it." George looked up and winked at me. "When you've solved this case, call them up and tell them you know an honest computer geek who can upgrade them to a state-of-the-art firewall—for a small price."

That's George for you.

"So what did you find?" I asked. George's methods sometimes make me nervous, but they don't upset me enough not to make use of any info she manages to dig up.

"Captain Mike Jones has had an interesting past. Look at this." George clicked to a page she'd bookmarked. Mike Jones's name came up. "See, he's been in trouble with the law before. The FBI snared him during a crackdown on smuggling out of New Orleans. Mike Jones owned a fishing excursion company some years back. Weird thing is, he was accused, but before he came to trial, the FBI dropped the charges."

"Not enough evidence?" Ned guessed.

"I can't seem to find out why. Hacking into FBI files will take a little longer—"

"I didn't hear that!" I protested, hands over my ears—but I continued to look over George's shoulder at the screen. Hey, it's irresistible. "Look, there's more on the captain."

"Right," George said, scanning the page. "Not long after the smuggling charges were dropped, he was hired on as the captain of a private yacht . . . which caught fire and sank under mysterious circumstances! I checked out the yacht's insurance company, and there were indications of insurance fraud. Again, no charges." She looked up. "Nancy, I swear you've got your man here."

"He *does* have a record . . . ," Ned added.

I shook my head. "Technically, he doesn't. Still, the guy's clearly been involved in shady dealings, one way or another. The fact that he just happened to be around when things went wrong on that yacht, or when the FBI came down on the smuggling ring, does seem like one too many coincidences."

"That's for sure," George insisted. "Oh, and there's some mystery involving his navy discharge. It was honorable, but I think a little sudden. I can't tell from these old files. There's so much blacked out in them."

I was as tempted as both George and Ned to jump to conclusions about Captain Mike. My sixth sense told me something about him was not what it seemed. I needed to find some better, harder evidence before I could begin to charge the captain of the ship with a crime.

Ned sensed my wariness. "Hey, I've got an idea. Since the FBI dropped the smuggling charges, maybe my dad can be of help here. You know, from when he was a journalist in DC. He made lots of contacts in the bureau." He pulled out his cell phone. "I'll phone him tonight and see what he can come up with. He's still probably at that conference."

11

Caught in the Act

But **if the captain's** got some criminal record," George wondered out loud, "it should turn up on that National Crime Fighters Database—which, by the way, I *could* hack into, but it'll take days. They've got notoriously great security."

In my concern about Ned, I had almost forgotten about the fax. "Captain Mike didn't mention if it had come in yet," I told her.

"Maybe he'd rather you didn't see what's on it," Ned suggested.

"And it isn't like Chief McGinnis to put off investigating the crew. You faxed Tonya hours ago," George said.

"*I* didn't fax her. The captain did. He has control over the only fax on the ship. I figured I'd stay close to him and the fax machine, just to be safe—but I've been so busy." Suddenly, Ned's comment made total sense. "What if Ned's right—Tonya faxed the info back here, and the captain is holding it?"

"Well, there's no way to find out without asking him," Ned said, getting up and heading for the door. He checked his watch. "It's past midnight and I'm turning in, but I'll ring your cell, Nancy, if Dad calls during the night with anything he's garnered from his contacts with the FBI."

George waited until Ned left to speak to me. "Nancy, where's the fax machine?"

"In the office, right off the wheelhouse."

She jumped off her bunk and rummaged in her knapsack. She pulled out a piece of Ready, Set, Eat! letterhead. "If you can get me access to the fax machine, I can find out when and *if* the captain actually sent the fax, and then if one came back."

"How?"

George wiggled her eyebrows.

"Okay. How will you get access to the fax machine to begin with?"

"With your help, and this letterhead. I'm going fax Mom's office. If anyone asks, I'll say something was missing from one of their deliveries to the ship. Not to worry."

George grabbed her small knapsack, and we both

headed for the wheelhouse, taking the stairs to the topmost deck two at a time.

The scheme went off without a hitch. Cab was alone in the wheelhouse, his injured leg propped up on a couple of cushions. While I inquired about his health and steered the conversation away from his bite and to dogs in general, George trotted into the office to send her fax. A moment later she poked her head out the door.

"Cab, where do you keep the spare film cartridges for this thing? The film's run out."

Cab tossed George a set of keys to the stationery supply cabinet, and we resumed our conversation. Two minutes later George came out of the office.

"Thanks, Cab," she said. "And I hope you feel better in the morning," she added, pointing to his leg.

"Aw, it's nothing. I've had worse than this before. One time an alligator . . . Eh, it's too late to get into *that* story." He stifled a yawn.

"Well, it's one I want to hear," I told him, relieved we wouldn't be held up in the office a minute longer and risk George being discovered with the old fax film. "Maybe in the morning."

With that, we left. Outside the office George whispered, "I've got it right here." She patted her backpack. "I'll work on it tonight." We headed down to the Plantation Deck together. While George continued farther down to the crew quarters, I went to my own cabin, retrieved my flashlight, changed my shoes, then descended the inside stairs to the dining room.

Safety lights illuminated the edges of the room. Not expecting anyone to be up this late, I walked right in—and stopped dead in my tracks. Fortunately the carpet muffled my footsteps. Right in front of my nose, up on the stage, two figures were creeping around the set in the dark. Each held a small pen-light, similar to the one I had in my pocket.

I observed them for a moment, then tiptoed over to the bar, leaned over the polished counter, and flicked on the overhead chandeliers.

"Nancy!" Toby Marchand exclaimed. The second figure, the woman with him, was Angela. At the sight of me her hand flew to her heart, and she sank down onto a sofa on the set and burst into tears.

"I didn't do it," she blubbered into her hands. "Really, it wasn't me."

I hadn't even blamed her yet, though it seemed pretty clear that Toby and Angela had just earned the top two spots on my list of suspects.

"Stop it, Angela," Toby ordered.

Amazingly she turned off the tears. But when she looked up at me, her face registered pure guilt. "I did not steal that necklace," she declared.

"Nancy hasn't even accused you. . . ."

"Yet," I added walking up to the stage. With a quick glance I checked the doors. The doors to the deck were all closed. The only way out of the dining room was past me. Good. I didn't want Toby or Angela to leave yet.

As I approached I noticed Angela was trying to cover something with her skirt. "What's that?" I pointed to the lump under the flowered cotton fabric.

Angela winced. "A box," she said, then pulled it out. It was wooden, and I recognized it as one of the props from the play.

I mounted the stage and held my hand out. She hesitated, then finally let it go. Before I could grab it, it slipped out of her hands and dropped onto the floor. The lid fell off, the bottom popped open, and something rattled out.

"A false bottom!" I cried, and then spotted something silver lying on the floor. Angela tried to cover it with her foot, but I was faster. I bent down and snatched it up. "Cassidy's locket?!"

Angela nodded, then burst into another round of tears.

Toby shook his head and walked up to her. I watched him hesitate before he finally put his arm around her shoulder. "Come on, Angela. It's over now. It's better everything's out in the open."

I waited for her to gather herself together enough

to confess to taking Mrs. Mahoney's necklace—and in the meantime I wondered about who her accomplice was. Toby? He'd been here during the whole play and blackout, though. There had to be another accomplice.

She kept sobbing, until finally my patience wore thin. "Angela, just tell me, where did you put the necklace?"

She looked up. Little rivulets of black mascara ran down her pretty face. "I—I didn't do it. I just took this locket because . . ." She looked at Toby, then threw herself back down on the couch and sobbed into her arms.

Toby groaned under his breath. "Nancy, I know what this looks like, but really it has nothing to do with Mrs. Mahoney. It's purely a company matter—"

"Toby there's been a crime onboard this ship," I said, struggling to keep my temper. "So there are no purely company matters. You know that."

Toby looked helplessly toward Angela, waiting for her to say something. She remained face down on the couch, but her shoulders were still. She had stopped sobbing and seemed to be listening to every word. Finally he threw up his hands. "It's about me and Cassidy. We're getting married at the end of this summer run. Angela's upset about it."

Angela suddenly jumped up. "You bet I am," she

said, facing Toby. "We'd been dating since January. Then this *old* flame turns up, and you drop me. Of course I'm upset. I'm beyond upset! That's why I took her 'lucky locket.'" Angela faced me and planted her hands on her hips, "I didn't steal it; I just hid it for a while. And it worked. Ever since, she can't even remember her lines. So much for you, *old* flame!"

"Don't be so mean," Toby protested—but not strongly enough, to my mind. Still, I had to believe her. And, though she might have had the opportunity during the blackout to steal the necklace, she didn't seem to have the steadiness of hand—or the nerve. Or the motive.

"So you believe us?" Toby said, coming down off the stage. Angela sank back down on the couch, grabbed a tissue from the box on the table, and loudly blew her nose.

I shrugged. "Yeah. But I can't say that makes me feel better—and you'd better do something about getting that locket back to Cassidy. Once Chief McGinnis hears about the missing locket and Angela's taking it, he's going to jump to conclusions." I handed him back the locket.

"I'll give it to Cassidy tonight. Actually I had my suspicions about Angela and the locket, but it wasn't until after our show tonight that she came to me and confessed, and begged me to come down here after hours with her while she got it. I was supposed to return it to Cassidy's bureau and make it look like it was lost all along."

"Okay," I said, then I remembered I wanted to check the flower arrangements. After Toby and Angela left, I started poking halfheartedly around the ones nearest the stage.

I was feeling frustrated and annoyed. I felt like I was in possession of the Incredible Shrinking List of Suspects. Every time I put someone on the list, within hours, even minutes, they got crossed off. Except for the mysterious Captain Mike.

A few hours later I woke to the insistent ringing of my cell phone. I surfaced groggily from the depths of a dream. It was a dream I didn't want to wake up from, because it held a clue. Something I should have remembered earlier in my investigation. But the minute I opened my eyes, all memories of the dream vanished.

I groped for the phone on the night table, and opened it to the incredibly cheerful sound of George's voice.

"Good morning!"

I rubbed the sleep from my eyes and groaned. I tipped open a slat in the shuttered cabin window. The sky was pink with dawn. "How can you sound so awake?"

"Because I haven't gone to bed yet. I pulled an all-nighter."

All at once I was wide awake. I swung my legs over the bed and sat up straight. "Did Tonya send a fax?"

"Did she ever! Turns out the crew is in the clear—with two possible exceptions."

"Interesting. What's Captain Mike's story?"

"He doesn't have one," George said. "Turns out when he faxed the crew's names to the chief, he left his own off. Can't swear that was on purpose, but . . ."

"Come off it, George. It *had* to be intentional. He's got that messy past! He knows once McGinnis reads about it, he'll decide the good captain's a suspect."

"Maybe," George said. "Mr. Nickerson's contacts might turn up something. But don't you want to hear about my other discovery?"

I began to pace the floor in my bare feet. "Out with it, George."

"Cab Mitchell also fell off the radar, so to speak, about fifteen years ago, when he left the navy. Then suddenly he turns up again about eight months ago. That's when he passed security clearance to work for this cruise operation," George said.

"But he *did* pass security clearance?" I wanted to be sure I'd heard right.

"Yeah—so I guess that rules him out," George concluded.

Hmm. I wasn't so sure of that. Fifteen years unaccounted for in a person's life . . . Where had he been? The first thing that leaped to my mind was jail. But then, his record would have shown up on the database.

Suddenly inspiration struck. "George, when you checked into the cruise company's records earlier, did it say who hired Cab?"

"Captain Mike," she answered. "He recommended him. They were in the same navy unit."

So they were old navy buddies! They probably had some interesting history together. Captain Mike's past, after the service, was shady. Was Cab's too? Had they somehow teamed up to be partners in crime? I decided to question the captain about his old friend . . . but carefully. I didn't want Captain Mike knowing that either he or Cab were under suspicion.

I ended the call, put away my phone, and headed straight for the shower. I was too revved up to even try to go back to bed. I'd take advantage of the early hour to do my morning jog around the deck.

I had just pulled on my running shorts and a sweatshirt when a woman's scream shattered the early-morning silence.

12

A Dastardly Deed

I raced for the door as the woman shrieked again. The cries were coming from the next cabin: Mrs. Mahoney's corner stateroom!

Still in a dressing gown, Mrs. Mahoney stood in the open doorway, pointing back into the stateroom. Other doors in the corridor flew open. People in various states of undress poked their heads out to see what had caused the commotion.

"Mrs. Mahoney, what's wrong?" I asked, then followed the direction of her pointing finger. At first I thought she was pointing to an off-white throw rug lying on the floor in front of her dressing table. And then I realized it wasn't a rug at all.

"Fizzy Lizzy!" I cried, and hurried over to the limp form. I stooped down. The dog's head lolled to one side, and her tongue hung limply out of the side of her mouth.

"Nancy, she's dead!" Mrs. Mahoney moaned in horror.

I looked up from the dog at Mrs. Mahoney. "Where's Ms. Tucker? And why's the dog here?"

"Nadine thought I should keep her overnight, because of the necklace being stolen and all. I went into the shower just now. And when I came out . . ." She broke off and turned as Ms. Tucker came into the room. Her eyes were heavy with sleep, and she was still tying her robe when she saw the limp form of the dog.

"Oh no!" she gasped, her hand flying to her mouth. "What happened?"

"I—I don't know. Oh Nadine, I feel so awful, I . . ."

I touched the dog's chest. "Ms. Tucker, I think she's still alive." I reached up for a compact lying on top of the dressing table. I opened it and held the mirror in front of the dog's mouth. Sure enough, it fogged over— the dog was still breathing. "She's just asleep. I think she'll be okay. But I think someone drugged her."

Mrs. Mahoney let out a small cry. "Who would do that?"

"And *how*?" Ms. Tucker wondered as Captain Mike walked in.

"What's happening here?" he asked, then saw

Fizzy Lizzy. "Something happened to the dog?"

"It didn't just happen," I told him. I rummaged through the wastepaper basket, then noticed a small foil packet—the kind single-dose medicine often comes in. It was open, and a pill had been pushed out from the other side. Half the pill had crumbled inside the packet. I realized the dog had only gotten half a dose of whatever the drug was.

"Here's the evidence," I said, gingerly picking up the packet.

Ms. Tucker looked at the pill. "Oh, I've seen that before. It's a common veterinary tranquilizer. Sometimes it's used during dog shows to calm the more nervous ones down between competitive events. I've used it when I've traveled with my dogs. But a whole pill like that is too much for this little pup. She'll be all right when she wakes up. It'll take a couple of hours, though."

"We'll never know if someone intended Fizzy Lizzy to take the whole pill, or knew enough to only give a small dog half the dose to knock her out," I said. As I spoke I massaged the dog's paws. She moaned slightly, and in her sleep, she licked my hand.

Privately I wondered if Cab was behind this.

"How did someone get into your room?" the captain asked Mrs. Mahoney.

"I—I don't know. I had locked the door, and I had

the door closed to the bathroom. I was taking my usual long morning bath. And when I came out, I found the poor creature like this. Oh, it was awful!"

"Who has keys to the door?" Ms. Tucker asked the captain, but I already was examining the lock.

"Someone jimmied this open. Look, the little bar is bent."

The captain apologized to Mrs. Mahoney for the lack of security, then left the two women to care for the dog.

I joined him in the hall. "Captain Mike, can I talk to you somewhere, in private?" Here was my chance to pump him for information about Cab, and maybe shed some light on his own past.

"Sure. I'd like to hear how the investigation's going," he said, leading the way outside.

I wasn't about to reveal that *he* was my prime suspect. First I asked if anyone in the crew had worked with a vet or with show animals. He didn't think so, though he had no way of knowing for sure. "Folks kind of gear their résumés to the jobs they're applying for," he said. "That kind of experience doesn't land them this kind of job." Then he thought a moment. "But maybe one of Toby's troop might have worked with animals."

I said I'd look into it, but privately I decided it wasn't worth my time. My gut told me Toby and his company were in the clear. Then I asked him about Nelson in the boiler room, and one or two names I noticed on the crew list—people I hadn't met yet. Trying not to rouse his suspicions, I saved questions about Cab until last.

"What's Cab's story?" I finally ventured. "He's an interesting guy."

Captain Mike readily agreed. "I've known him since we were kids—your age, actually. We sailed the same carrier in the navy, and ended up bunking together our last tour of duty."

"And what did he do after the navy?"

Captain Mike pushed his cap back on his head and leaned against the rail. "Lots of things, I reckon. I sort of lost touch with him within a year or two. . . . That's how things go sometimes. Then he turned up, oh, six months or so ago, down in New Orleans and needing work. I hired him in a flash. He's a darn good pilot and a worthy seaman. One of the few people I'd trust this boat to in a pinch."

Hearing the captain admit he couldn't account for the gap in Cab's life made me wonder. Was the captain covering for the two of them? Or had he honestly lost track of an old friend?

I waited a moment or two, then asked as casually as I could, "Why was such a good sailor out of work?"

"Cab became a shrimper down in the gulf. He

had his own ship, apparently. The shrimp catch has been going down for a while now. Times were bad, then his boat was wrecked when it tried to make for port ahead of a hurricane. That was last year. His insurance couldn't cover the damages, and then on top of that, he got injured."

"Right, his cane."

"Makes it hard to get hired these days. Lots of able-bodied men looking for work. But I wouldn't let an old friend down. Besides, I have enough young muscle on this ship to handle what he can't." The captain made a face. "That's one reason I took on Dylan. He's nice enough, but hopeless when it comes to machinery. Fortunately he's got some muscle on him, which comes in handy when we need help." Then the captain smiled to himself. "And then, this spring Cab told me about his niece needing a summer job. So I hired her, and she's been great with the guests. She gets along with the crew and has already learned everything about the boat. She's got a knack for sailing, all right. A regular old salt she is . . . without looking like one, I might add."

"Who's his niece?"

"That redheaded waitress. The looker. Hillary."

"Captain Mike to the bridge. Captain Mike to the bridge," a voice called over the ship's intercom.

"I guess you'll have to catch me up on the investigation later," the captain said with a frown. "I'm expecting a call from McGinnis to give him our estimated time of arrival."

He left me feeling stumped. If Cab was an unemployed shrimper, how come his previous boat and the wreck didn't leave a paper trail of some sort? I thought all shipwrecks, even those involving the smallest craft, were subject to Coast Guard investigation.

On the other hand, maybe like lots of other people on the financial fringe of things, he worked off the books. Maybe he really never had insurance for his boat. Then I remembered the captain's connection to smugglers, and the hint of his involvement in insurance fraud. Were the two of them working together?

I grabbed a breakfast bar from one of the baskets of goodies that were conveniently located on tables around the deck. I was still pondering the captain's story when Ned found me settled in a chair on the Plantation Deck, finishing the last of my breakfast.

"Nancy, you're not going to believe this," he said, pulling over one of the deck chairs. He sat down facing me. His eyes were shining with excitement.

I knew instantly he had some kind of big news. "You heard from your dad."

He nodded. "And this is really over the top!" He beckoned me to lean in closer. Lowering his voice, he said, "Our good Captain Mike hasn't fallen off the radar. The radar's been ordered to ignore his very existence! He's undercover, Nancy. For the FBI. Dad couldn't find out much more than that, but I don't think he's one of the bad guys here."

"You mean he wasn't one of the smugglers, but was working for the Feds?"

Ned nodded. "But you don't look like it's good news."

"It is for the captain. Not for *my* latest theory." I told him about the shrimper and Cab's past.

I was about to launch into the details of the shipwreck when I heard the tap of a cane. I looked up, and Cab was headed our way.

"Morning," Cab said.

"How's the leg?" Ned asked. I wondered if he had heard about the dog being drugged. I was also wondering if Cab had tried to do the animal in.

"I'll live," he answered. "I've been through worse, though I think that dog's dangerous and should be put to sleep. That's what I think."

Put to sleep? Interesting. I made a mental note.

"Oh, Cab, you're overreacting," Ned said. "She was excited from the performance, and something about you or your cane scared her. She's just high-strung."

"Yeah, you can say that again." Cab looked at me and brightened. "Hi, Nancy. Any progress on your case?"

"Some," I felt safe saying. "I was talking with the

captain, and he told me you used to own a shrimper!"

Cab's eyes widened slightly. "Oh, he told you all about that?"

"And that it was wrecked."

Cab tapped his leg gently with his cane. "That's how come I've got this limp and need the cane."

Ned looked interested. "What was the name of the boat?"

He hesitated a second before answering. "The *Ebony Sunset*." After Cab said good-bye, I told Ned I'd see him at lunch. Then I went down to George's room. I filled her in on Cab's story and asked her to check out a shrimper called the *Ebony Sunset*.

"No such ship," she declared a little while later. There was no record of a shrimper by that name . . . of *any* boat by that name. No shipwreck off the coast of New Orleans, and no insurance records.

"That leaves Cab with some explaining to do," I told her.

George frowned. "Nancy, I'd be careful here. If this guy can cover his tracks so completely, he's no amateur. He's connected to bigger fish somehow. I'm sure of it."

"I'm not sure about being connected to other thieves—but I agree, he's probably slightly dangerous. Don't worry. I'll be careful. Anyway, as far as I know, he hasn't a clue that I'm on to him."

13

Steamed

I know I probably should have told George that the minute I left her cabin I was going to look for Cab. I wasn't going to confront him, just try to feel him out some more. I wasn't completely convinced he was the bad guy here—though I had no other likely suspect on my list. But if he was the thief, then why did he openly express his desire to see that dog killed? Wouldn't that cast suspicions on him for (1) poisoning the animal and, more to the point, (2) breaking into Mrs. Mahoney's cabin, perhaps in search of more jewels?

While I was tracking down Cab, I came across Dylan and Bess. They were painting a couple of wooden rocking chairs. When I walked up, they were, as usual, arguing. I wondered how Bess would handle this for the rest of her internship. At the moment Bess looked like she'd welcome the chance to bow out of this gig and get back to her own projects.

"Hi, guys," I greeted them a little warily. "What's going on?"

"*We* seem to have broken one of the chairs," Bess remarked.

Dylan obligingly held up the rocker that had fallen off the base of the chair. "It's old. The glue's dried out." He turned to Bess and added pointedly, "You see, even a mechanical idiot like yours truly knows there's glue holding together parts of these rocking chairs."

I didn't know what to say.

"Some people think when things break, you just toss them. That's not good for the environment, Nancy, is it?" Bess asked with exaggerated sweetness.

"Um—no, it's good to re-use things when you can. Anyway, I have to go and get a hold of—"

Dylan didn't give me a chance to finish my sentence. "But it would save lots of time and energy—and in this case, paint—to just toss it."

"Look, you don't have to expend any time and energy. I'm going to bring this down to the workshop later and glue it together. . . ."

Without saying good-bye, I continued on my quest to find Cab.

For some reason, today he was elusive. Someone told me he was in the wheelhouse, but when I got there, Captain Mike said the first mate was in the Observation Lounge working with some charts. But the lounge was empty.

When I checked the dining room, Ken mentioned Cab was looking for Nelson down in engineering.

Downstairs the door to the boiler room was open. I ventured in. I didn't see Cab or Nelson. "Anyone here?" I yelled over the noise of the boiler.

"In here, Nancy!" Bess called from the direction of the wood shop.

"Have you seen Cab?" I asked, venturing inside. Dylan was stowing paint cans on a high shelf. The broken rocker was propped on a workbench. Bess was busy clamping the curved rocker to the legs of the chair. "There," she said, wiping her hands on a rag. "It'll sit like this for twenty-four hours, and then it'll be good as new."

"Whatever," Dylan grumbled. "I'm hungry. It's gotta be time for lunch." He went over to the sink and washed his hands. I noticed sweat pouring down the back of his neck. Then I realized I was sweating too.

"It's hot in here!" I said.

"Always is," Dylan replied.

Bess made a face. "Not this hot." She walked into

the boiler room. A moment later she yelled, "Nancy, come here! Something's wrong."

I hurried into the boiler room. The heat suddenly seemed suffocating, and the boiler was making a strange rumbling noise.

"Look at these gauges," she said. "The pressure in this first boiler is building too high."

"The safety valve will kick in," Dylan said, still drying his hands with a towel. When he finished, he draped it around his neck.

But even as I looked at the gauge, the needle was creeping very close to the red danger zone. "Shouldn't it have kicked in by now?" I asked, wiping the beads of sweat off my forehead.

Bess nodded. "Where's Nelson? He's supposed to be on duty."

"I didn't see him when I came in," I answered.

Bess went around to the other side of the array of boilers. I followed and watched as she began to check the maze of pipes. "Something's wrong here, Nancy. This steam-release valve looks like it's jammed or something." She tried to touch it, but drew her hand back quickly. "Too hot!" she said. "I'm not sure how to get it to release—"

"You shouldn't even try," Dylan spoke up from behind us. I turned. He looked nervous. "Don't you remember, Bess? Cab told us the steam in here would leave you with third-degree burns at the very least. We need to get help."

I agreed and had Dylan show me the intercom. I pressed the button, but nothing happened. "Hey, anyone listening? There's a problem in the boiler room." I waited a few seconds, but no one answered.

"What's this?" Dylan asked, holding out the frayed end of a wire. The other end of the wire was connected to the base of the intercom.

The wire had been cut. Someone had sabotaged the intercom!

"I'll run upstairs and tell someone." I said. "Maybe you guys should get out of here though. Just in case—"

"Just in case it blows!" Dylan exclaimed. He started with me for the door, then turned and looked for Bess. "Bess, let's get out of here!" he yelled. When she didn't answer, he hurried back behind the boilers to look for her.

When I reached the door, it was closed, and the handle didn't budge. I tried again, but the door wouldn't open. For a moment I thought it was because of the heat, and then I realized what had happened. "Someone's locked the door!" I cried.

Dylan raced over—thankfully, with Bess, who had been behind the boilers trying to figure out a solution—and began tugging on the handle. "I don't get it," he said, looking at me. "The only way this locks is with a key."

"Someone locked us in on purpose," Bess exclaimed. "We've got to get out of here, Nancy, fast. That safety valve is stuck. The whole ship will blow up if we can't turn down the steam."

Suddenly Dylan grabbed my arm. "Did you hear that?"

"What?" Bess asked.

"I heard a thumping noise. . . ."

"Dylan," Bess wailed, "this isn't time for jokes."

That's when I heard it too—a noise coming from the storage room. "He's not joking. What's in there?" I asked, hurrying over to the door. I lifted the latch and threw open the storage-room door.

Nelson stumbled out. His workshirt was filthy, and he looked sick.

"Ooooh, my head," he moaned, sinking down on the nearest stool. As he passed me I got a whiff of a sickeningly familiar odor.

"Ether!" I gasped. Someone had knocked Nelson out with an anesthetic. "Nelson." I shook his shoulder. "Who did this to you?"

He looked at me, bleary eyed. It took a moment for him to focus on my face. "I feel so sick," he mumbled.

"You're going to feel *beyond* sick if you don't pull yourself together," Dylan said, shaking him.

"The boiler," Bess interjected, shaking his shoulders. "Nelson, listen to me. The pressure's going out of control. The release valve is jammed. We need help here! NOW!"

I yanked the towel off Dylan's neck and ran to the water cooler. I doused the towel in cold water, then went back and put it over Nelson's face. "Wake up, Nelson. This is serious."

The cold damp towel did the trick. Slightly revived, Nelson stood up. His walk was a bit wonky, but he managed to follow Bess over to the pressure-release valve.

"Hey, this thing's been capped!" he exclaimed.

Bess looked at the pipe he was pointing to and paled. "Nancy, I bought a cap just like this yesterday at the hardware store. It was on my shopping list."

14

Dead in the Water

You bought that cap?" Nelson stared at her. "Why?"

"Like I said, it was on the list." Bess's bottom lip began to quaver.

"There's no time to worry about this now. Nelson, what do we do?"

The crewman rubbed his hand across his forehead. "Let me think . . . my brain's all full of cotton wool. What did that guy do to me, anyway? Wait—what we've got to do is cut off the fuel supply to the boilers. Where's my walkie-talkie?" He felt his pockets and didn't come up with it.

"Whoever cut the intercom wires probably took it," I realized with dismay.

"No, no they didn't," Nelson said, stumbling over to the desk. "It's right here." He switched it on and contacted the pilot house, warning them he was going to cut the fuel supply to the engines. "And send someone down here. . . . They tell me the boiler-room door is locked from the outside. We've got a major problem, Captain Mike. Hurry."

He disappeared into another part of the engine room, Bess in tow. A few minutes later he came back with a tool box. I watched him check the pressure gauge. Sure enough, it was slowly dropping back from the danger zone. "It'll take a while for the pressure to drop back to normal. But meanwhile, the ship will stand still in the water."

Dylan shook his head. "Who would do this?"

"Someone who wanted the boat to stop before getting back to River Heights," I guessed.

"Cab's going to hate this," Nelson said as Dylan brought him water from the cooler. "He hates having to start the boat up from a stall like this. We do have backup power. But even getting that online takes time."

"Speaking of Cab," I spoke up, "where is he? Someone told me he was down here."

"He left a few minutes before I was knocked out. He was doing something over there at the other desk, then his beeper went off. I headed into the storage room, and he headed back to the pilot house."

"Did you guys see him leave?" I asked Bess.

"No—and I didn't see him come in, either. We were in the workshop fixing that rocker. I didn't hear a thing until you turned up."

Suddenly the door to the boiler room burst open. Cane and all, Cab barreled through. He looked horrified. "What in the world happened here?" he bellowed. "You kids okay?"

The captain was right behind him, fuming. Now that I knew he was one of the good guys, I was beyond happy to see him. I felt safer knowing he was on board this ship "This is intolerable," he cried. "A missing necklace is one thing, but the whole ship could have been blown to smithereens. People might have been killed! I'm calling McGinnis now. I want police presence. I want this case solved." He glared at me—and for once, I didn't mind. I wished I could tell him that I was almost sure of my suspect, but I still didn't have enough hard evidence. And I wanted confirmation that the people on board would be safe.

"So, how did you end up locked in here?" the captain asked me.

"I came down here looking for Cab." Then I asked Cab directly. "Where were you? Nelson said you were here right before someone knocked him out with an anesthetic."

"Nelson got knocked out?" Cab limped over to the engineer. "Hey, man, you okay?"

Nelson nodded. "Now I am. That was a close call, Cab. Another five or ten minutes and that boiler would have blown."

"I hear you, I hear you," Cab commiserated. Then he turned back to me. "I left here to go up to the pilot house. I didn't get there right away. I stopped at Hillary's cabin—you know she's my niece, don't you?" he asked me.

"The captain told me," I answered, then pursued my questioning. "And you didn't see anyone else down here?"

"Not a living soul."

15

The Missing Link

So there we were, the *Magnolia Belle* dead in the water, and me without enough evidence to prove my case. How would I ever convince Chief McGinnis that Cab Mitchell was somehow behind the robbery, and all the subsequent incidents? A piece of the puzzle was missing, and I had the distinct feeling I was staring right at it.

I needed to brainstorm with my friends, but Bess was stuck working with Dylan, and George was in the kitchen with her mom. Thoughts of Mrs. Fayne, George, and the kitchen made me realize that since last night's dinner, I'd had only a breakfast bar. It was midafternoon, and I was starving. Maybe if I rummaged through the galley's fridge and pantry, I could come up with a proper snack and sound out George at the same time.

It was a plan, and it worked. Half an hour after leaving the boiler room, while the off-duty crew and waitstaff had lunch in the dining room, I was huddling with George in the pantry, devouring a sandwich. "So the problem is," I told her between bites, "I'm sure Cab's involved—but I can't make the case that he was. First of all, he wasn't in the dining room when the jewelry went missing."

"And," George pointed out, "if poisoning the dog was part of a plot to steal more jewels from Mrs. Mahoney, then it couldn't have been Cab."

"Why?"

"Because the very sight of Cab would send that dog into a barking fit loud enough to wake the dead."

"So the second thief—or accomplice, or partner—doesn't scare the dog, and can move quietly—"

"And quickly," George finished my thought.

I sighed, then threw my paper plate in the garbage can next to the pantry counter. I rewrapped the half of baguette left over from making my lunch and went to put it in the bread box. As I opened it, something caught my eye. A sheet of paper was stuck between the back of the stainless-steel box and the wall. I pulled the box away from the wall and retrieved the paper. It was a large sheet, eleven by seventeen inches. It was filled with circles and names and numbers.

"Funny, that's a seating diagram," George said, looking over my shoulder.

"Right, for the Whodunit Dinner." I started to throw it out, and then I noticed the diagram had Mrs. Mahoney's table front row—but at the other side of the stage. Her final table assignment had been switched. Ken had mentioned it was Hillary who reconstructed the seating assignments. Shifting Mrs. Mahoney's table from the right side of the room to the left might have been an innocent—and certainly easy—mistake to make. But there was something else I remembered about Hillary that made me sure the switch around was no mistake.

"George," I said as I made my way out of the kitchen. "I think I've got it. I have a hunch I know who's working with Cab!"

"Where are you going, Nancy?" George called after me.

I didn't bother to answer. Either this hunch would pay off, or it wouldn't. In either case I had to find Hillary's room while the waitstaff and crew were in the dining room, still eating.

I knew her room was on the lower deck, only a few doors down from George's. I tried the handle, but the door was locked. Reaching in my pocket for my wallet, I pulled out a credit card. Carefully I slid the card between the lock and the side of the door. The bolt gave way immediately.

Hillary's room looked like any college girl's dorm room. Posters plastered on every wall. At first that seemed perfectly normal, until I realized these weren't usual dorm-room posters—no movie posters, no posters of rock stars. Hillary's preference was for circus posters. I walked up and took a closer look. Every one of the posters was from the same circus troupe: Bartholomew and Bartlett's Traveling Circus. Small print revealed the circus was based in New Orleans. The circus logo was the grimacing head of a clown—the same clown tattooed on Cab's leg. Cab was part of this circus, but for whatever reason he omitted any mention of it on his résumé. And several of the posters featured a small white dog: "The Amazing Delta, the Death Defying Wonder Beast." Delta—wasn't that what Cab had called Fizzy Lizzy when she bit him?

Trying to work fast, I went through Hillary's drawers and found nothing. Then I noticed the old-fashioned steamer trunk at the foot of her bed. I knelt down and opened it. The top tray held a ton of programs and flyers and newspaper clippings. All featured the same circus, in various venues, all in the Deep South, but mainly for small towns in Louisiana and Alabama. I scanned the programs looking for Cab Mitchell's name. He wasn't mentioned any-where.

Puzzled, I lifted out the top tray. Underneath were a couple of exotic Middle Eastern dance-type costumes with chiffon pantaloons and sequined tops. They looked like they'd all fit Hillary—and in fact, she'd look great in them. There were several colorful programs with drawings of a Hillary look-alike named Helena who was part of a magic act.

Helena was probably Hillary's stage name.

The one clue I kept forgetting had been right in front of my nose: Hillary knew magic tricks. I'd even seen her work one with that kid the day before on the pier. And Hillary had been in the dining room when the necklace was stolen.

I carefully peeked beneath the costumes. At the very bottom of the trunk I spied a pile of newspaper clippings. I took them out and riffled through them. They were neatly stacked in order of date. I started reading the earliest ones from about nine months ago first.

Apparently Bartholomew and Bartlett's Traveling Circus had suffered some sort of minor tragedy. There'd been an accident. A man named Callum Moore had sustained a leg injury when a fire swept through one of the circus's sideshow tents. The loss to the circus was enormous, and there was talk of its disbanding.

I reread the article and suddenly realized that Callum Moore's left leg was injured—and so was Cab's. Cab had an alias: Callum Moore! That's why Cab Mitchell vanished. Since he left the navy, he'd been living under an assumed name—maybe several assumed names. I began to wonder what George might find if she plugged Callum Moore into her search engine.

Eagerly I read the next batch of articles, all dated beginning a month or so later. Apparently every town Bartholomew and Bartlett's opened in experienced a series of high-end jewelry heists. No connection was made at first to the presence of the circus personnel, for none of the victims had ever been to a Bartholomew and Bartlett's show. But when the string of robberies stopped, the authorities came to two conclusions: Someone who was no longer with the circus had been part of the burglary ring, and that same someone was connected to a wider national, and perhaps international, network of jewel thieves—because the stolen goods began turning up in New York and London, at major auction houses.

I didn't need to read more. I started to put the newspapers back in the trunk. Then I noticed a white envelope, about two by four inches, at the very bottom of the trunk. I picked it up. Stamped on the outside was the name of a New Orleans veterinarian. Inside were two white pills in foil packets. They looked like the same sort of pill I'd found in the wastebasket in Mrs. Mahoney's room.

George was right. Cab couldn't have poisoned the dog. And now I knew it had to have been Hillary. For some reason the animal trusted Hillary and hated Cab. I shuddered when I started imagining why. Cab had, for a moment, shown a really cruel streak toward animals. If he had been involved in Delta/Fizzy's training, the dog probably loathed him!

I started to close the trunk, when suddenly I felt something hard and cold pressed against the back of my neck. "Don't move," a woman's voice ordered.

It was Hillary. "Now get up slowly."

"Hillary," I said, starting to turn around. She shoved me back down to my knees. But before I stumbled down on the floor, I saw what I needed to see: It wasn't a gun pressed to my skin, it was the neck of a glass soda bottle, cold from the vending machine. I forced myself to calm down. I could deal with a woman with a soda bottle in her hand. I just had to plan my move carefully. First things first: keep her talking.

"Hillary, I figured it all out. You and your uncle

stole Mrs. Mahoney's necklace. Problem is, you won't get away with it." I was bluffing, of course. Though George was aware I suspected Cab, she had no idea about Hillary's role in the theft.

"But I *have* gotten away with it, and so has Cab. By the way, I will admit you're pretty good to have figured all this out. But you're wrong on one point: Cab isn't my uncle. He's just the muscle man in the operation—the guy with the know-how, like how to rig a boiler, or cause the right kind of blackout at the proper moment. I used my beeper. Like this." She stopped to press it, and I assumed she was beeping Cab. She continued to brag. "I was in the dining room, of course. He was down in engineering."

"So his limp is fake?"

"Nope. He really did get hurt that last gig outside of Baton Rouge. He's damaged goods, but my uncles—my *real* uncles—think he's still valuable."

While she talked, I managed to face her. I was still sitting. I saw she was gloating, and I watched as slowly her hand holding the Coke bottle began to relax. I took a deep breath, and as she started to tell me the details of how she stole the necklace, I jumped up.

I aimed a kick at her head, taking her off guard. She lost her balance—only for a minute. The next second she was blocking my moves, and I realized she knew what she was doing. We struggled, but finally I pinned her facedown to the floor. I had to sit on her back to keep her still.

"Come on, give up, Hillary," I said.

Before I could say more, the door flew open behind me, hitting me in the back of the head. For a moment I saw stars and lost my grip on Hillary. She pounced on me and yanked my arms behind my back.

Cab limped into the cabin, locking the door behind him. I squirmed, trying to get free of Hillary.

Cab raised his cane over my head. "Now, little Miss Detective, if you're all as smart as you're cracked up to be, you'll be quiet and do as I say. Get up, sit on that chair, and keep your mouth shut."

Hillary pulled me to my feet and shoved me onto the chair.

"Cab, this is crazy. Stealing a necklace is one thing. Assault is another. You're going to get caught and end up doing hard time," I warned.

"Maybe, maybe not. But you're not going to have much to do with it one way or the other." Turning to Hillary he said, "Tie her hands behind her back."

Hillary pulled a scarf out of a drawer and bound my wrists. When she finished, Cab ordered, "Go to my cabin. Inside my footlocker you'll find a small glass bottle. Bring it and a small towel."

She left, and he continued, "You're getting to be a

big problem, Nancy Drew. We're going to have to do something about this."

"They'll find that necklace eventually," I taunted, hoping he'd let on where he'd hidden it.

"I doubt it. Even you don't have a clue where it's stashed."

Within minutes Hillary returned. I spotted the bottle in her hand and realized what Cab intended to do. My heart began to race. I needed to get out of this room fast. "Come on, Cab. Don't do this," I told him.

He came toward me anyway.

"Hold her down," he told Hillary.

"With pleasure," Hillary responded, and gripped my shoulders hard. I watched in horror as Cab opened the bottle, then soaked the towel in foul-smelling liquid. I opened my mouth and started to scream, but instantly Cab muffled my mouth with one hand, then shoved the towel over my face. The odor overwhelmed me, and my stomach started to rebel. I fought back the sick feeling, determined not to give in to the anesthetic.

Trying not to breathe, I kicked. I heard Cab yelp. Someone kicked my right shin, but I barely felt the pain. The last thing I remember is Cab's mocking tone: "Sweet dreams . . ."

Then nothing.

16

Overboard

It was the steady, rhythmic pounding in my skull that woke me.

I tried to open my eyes, but the lids felt like lead weights. Where was I? Not at home in bed, that was for sure. The air against my skin was cool and damp. Something hard and rough pressed against my spine. I had the mother of all headaches, and the pounding seemed to be coming from inside and outside my body, like surround sound.

My head wasn't just pounding—it felt tender. Like I'd hit it on something. But what? I went to touch my forehead and realized I couldn't move my hands. My fingers closed around a silky scarf. Touching the scarf, I suddenly remembered everything: Hillary's cabin, the circus posters, realizing that Hillary and

Cab were a team of thieves and con artists, and then Cab coming at me with an ether-soaked rag. They'd knocked me out, then dragged me somewhere. They'd also stuffed a gag in my mouth.

Ether—that explained the nausea and the headache. But the pounding that happened with every noise? I focused on the sound. It was a familiar soft *chug-a-chug-a*.

I had to *see* where I was. Opening my eyes kicked my headache up a notch, but I fought back the nausea. Even with my eyes wide open, I couldn't see any-thing—just darkness. I was inside a closed space, look-ing up at the dark underside of . . . I blinked a few times and let my sight adjust to the dark. A tarp. Wherever I was, it was covered by a tarp.

A *tarp*? Suddenly I knew exactly where I was: the *chug-a-chug-a* was the sound of the *Magnolia Belle*'s engines. They had been fired up again, which meant that I had been knocked out for hours. I had gone to Hillary's cabin in the afternoon, and now it was night. That's why the air was cool and damp. Fog had moved in, and we were on our way back to River Heights with me inside one of the *Belle*'s lifeboats.

Hillary and Cab had stashed me here. They'd probably made their getaway by now, but if I could get out of this boat, I'd be able to report them to

Chief McGinnis and the captain—maybe in time to catch them.

I wriggled across the bottom of the lifeboat toward one of the oarlocks. Then I sat up, my head grazing the bottom of the tarp. After a few failed attempts, I managed to get my wrists over the lock. I snared the scarf and pulled hard. There was a ripping sound as the fabric tore, leaving my hands free.

I yanked the gag out of my mouth and was about to yell for help when I heard Cab's voice.

I froze. Why was he still on board?

He was talking to someone. At first he spoke so softly I couldn't make out the words, but as he drew closer, I heard him say, "We'll lower the boat now. We're not that far from the island."

"Uncle Jake and Pete C. will be waiting."

So Hillary was still on board too, and they planned to make their getaway in *this* boat. My heart froze in my chest. Somehow I had to get out of the boat and get help. Then I realized Hillary was still talking. "I hope they're not ticked off. That Drew girl managed to throw a wrench in this operation. I really think we should just get rid of her."

"Forget about it! We're leaving her on the island, safe and sound. Someone will find her sooner, or hopefully, later," Cab exclaimed. "Robbery's one thing. Murder's another. I don't kill people."

"Not intentionally." Hillary's voice oozed sarcasm.

"Yeah, well . . . accidents happen."

"Like that fire at the circus. Two people, dead. Like my uncle said, if you get caught, you're up for at least some kind of manslaughter or felony murder."

"*If* . . . That's a big two-letter word. I have no intention of getting caught. No *if.* So let's get our act on the road"—Cab laughed—"or on the river, as the case may be."

I knew I had to make my move—it was now or never. I grabbed one end of the tarp and flung it off, hoping it would fall over Cab and Hillary's heads. Then I tried to jump out of the lifeboat. Unfortunately my legs were limp as noodles: the aftereffect of the ether. As I flung myself toward the deck, I landed right in Cab Mitchell's brawny arm.

"Look what we have here," Cab said, clapping a hand over my mouth. I mumbled and fought against him. Then I tried going limp. "That-a-girl. No point fighting me now."

"So now what?" Hillary said. I detected a note of panic in her voice. "There's no time to tie her up. We can't hang around here on deck forever. People will finish their dinner soon and—"

"And Nancy here just got herself out of the frying pan and is headed right for the fire. Or rather, the river."

"But her arms are free. She overheard everything, Cab. We should tie her up so she can't swim."

"No time for that now. Besides, swimming will be the least of her problems." He pulled a bandanna out of his pocket with one hand, then stuffed it in my mouth with the other. Grabbing me under my arms, he told Hillary, "Get her legs and follow me."

Kicking and struggling, I tried to yell in spite of my gag. Where was everyone, anyway? All my efforts proved fruitless. I was too weak—and the two of them were too strong.

They carried me back toward the stern of the ship, then stopped at the railing. "On the count of three," he said to Hillary.

"One . . . two . . . three."

They swung me high out over the water and heaved me overboard.

17

Secrets in the Sand

I landed in the water with a splash and fought my way to the surface, kicking off my sneakers. I struggled to catch my breath, but already the shock of cold river water had snapped me out of any lingering grogginess. I treaded the frothy water and struggled out of my sweatshirt. That left me in my running shorts and a tank top. At least my clothing wouldn't weigh me down.

For the span of about five seconds, I almost felt like cheering. If Cab Mitchell thought he'd silence me by dumping me overboard, he was in for the surprise of his life. My form may not be good, but I'm a strong long-distance swimmer.

I wiped the water from my face and got my bearings. I was on the ship's port side, farthest from land.

When I looked toward the front of the *Belle*, I saw that the lifeboat was just hitting the water. Cab loosened the ropes that had lowered the boat from the deck. He handed an oar to Hillary, then eased himself to the seat in the stern.

Watching him, I realized I had two options: make for the *Belle* and shimmy up the ropes to reach the deck and get help—or swim after the lifeboat. I could probably follow it the whole way back to Stony Lonesome Island. But before I could make a decision, Cab dropped something off the back of the lifeboat. A second later I heard the whirr of an outboard motor.

He brought the lifeboat around and sped upstream.

Okay. So I'd get back on board the *Belle* and call for help. I'd get some pretty nasty rope burns on my legs in the process, and probably wreck my clothes, but really, this was the least of my worries.

It seemed no matter how hard I swam toward the front of the boat, I was being pulled back toward the stern. I'd never swum that stretch of the Muskoka before, and the current was strong—stronger than it should have been.

Suddenly, to my horror, I realized why. The combination of the boat plowing forward through the water and the action of the paddle wheel made the water doubly treacherous here.

Cab had purposely thrown me over toward the back of the boat. He figured I'd go under, and then surface right beneath the big wooden blades of the paddle wheel.

The realization kicked me into high gear. I gritted my teeth and began to swim as hard as I could, not up toward the prow of the boat, but out away from it, toward the center of the river. For a moment my efforts felt hopeless, then suddenly I realized I was slowly making headway. Slowly, slowly I made progress, into calmer waters.

The moment I did, the beam of a giant searchlight swept the surface of the river. The light blinded me, but made me want to cheer. There was only one light like that in River Heights—it belonged to the police department's river rescue crew. I pumped one arm in the air and waved and yelled. "Over here!"

Sure enough, within moments the rescue boat had pulled up. I was shocked to see Chief McGinnis among the officers onboard. Officer Joe Rees was there too, along with Sergeant Emily Kim and some other officer I didn't recognize. The chief helped haul me out of the river, and I actually saw a flash of real concern sweep across his face. It lasted about thirty seconds as he threw a rough army blanket over my shoulders. To my surprise, I was actually shivering.

"Where'd you come from?" I sputtered.

Officer Rees grinned. "When you went missing, Captain Mike radioed the chief for help."

Chief McGinnis grunted. "Nancy, you're the last person I thought I'd be fishing out of here tonight. What mess have you gotten yourself in this time?" he asked as the police boat turned around and raced back toward the *Belle*.

I didn't bother to answer that. Though my teeth were chattering, I blurted out, "It's Cab—Cab Mitchell and Hillary Duval. They're a pair of jewel thieves and con artists."

"You caught them with the necklace?"

I shook my head. "No. They've got it stowed somewhere. But even as we speak, they're headed off in one of the *Belle*'s lifeboats to Stony Lonesome Island. They're hooking up with Hillary's uncle Jake, and some guy named Pete C. I overheard them making plans."

"Jake *Duval*?" Officer Rees whistled beneath his breath. "He's connected to that Tarkovsky mob back East."

"Tough stuff. And I think we all know about Pete C.," said Chief McGinnis.

I didn't, but I figured this wasn't the time to ask too many questions. Suddenly I realized we had almost reached the boat. A half an hour ago, the deck seemed deserted, but it was crowded now. I made out Ned hanging over the railing, gesturing wildly at me, and then George and Bess, and Mrs. Mahoney. Next to her was Ms. Tucker, with Delta/Fizzy Lizzy tucked under one arm.

I waved up at all of them, then I realized what the chief was saying. "I'll get you back on board, and then send a detail to the island."

"No!" I shouted. "You can't do that. We've got to go to the island now." Maybe because I jumped up in the boat, or because I yelled and my voice carried, Fizzy Lizzy suddenly leaped out of Ms. Tucker's arms. The dog hurled herself over the railing and landed in the water just shy of our outboard motor.

"My dog!" Ms. Tucker shrieked. But the words were barely out of her mouth when Officer Rees leaned over and scooped the bedraggled creature out of the river. The dog shook herself, then hurled her body at me and began licking my face.

"What's this about?" the chief asked, clearly confused.

I wasn't sure, and at the moment the dog was the least of our worries. "Look, Chief. I'm fine. Every minute we waste here gives Cab and Hillary more time to get to the island and their accomplices. I'm sure they've got a getaway planned."

"She's right, Chief," the officer piloting the boat

144

spoke up. "Look." He pointed upstream at the swiftly vanishing lights of the lifeboat.

"Okay, Nancy. You win. But when we get there, you're to stay in this boat with that dog. And that's an order."

I had no choice but to promise him I'd stay put.

Once we reached the island, I tried to keep my word. The police anchored the boat in the shallows just offshore. The lifeboat was nowhere in sight. They headed off, leaving me and Fizzy Lizzy on board with some water and an emergency lantern.

Now, I'm a girl who usually keeps promises. So what happened next was really the dog's fault. And that's the truth.

All four officers waded through the shallows and hurried down the beach toward the forest and the western side of the island—a wooded area with a deep sheltered cove. A logical hiding place for a boat.

The moon was high in the sky, and I kept my eye trained on the beach. In my experience, criminals didn't usually act according to police logic. Suddenly Fizzy Lizzy let out a low growl.

"Hey, what's up?" I whispered, tightening my grip on her collar.

She growled again. Suddenly she bolted out of my grasp. She splashed into the water, then dog-paddled toward shore. What choice did I have? I had to go after her. Grabbing the emergency lantern, I climbed into the shallow water and walked to the shore.

She was already on the sandy beach, shaking the water off her back. Then she trotted with great deliberation toward the bluffs and caves on the eastern side of the island.

Hampered by my bare feet, I made slow progress over the sand and up through the woods, praying with every step that there was no poison ivy.

There was, however, a path. It was narrow, but by moonlight it was easy to follow. It twisted around some large boulders, then suddenly opened up at the foot of the bluffs. I found myself in front of Luther's famous caves.

Fizzy Lizzy had gotten there first. The dog was planted in front of one of the caves, barking, growling, and crouching as if ready to attack. Her behavior was a dead giveaway as to who was inside. So I wasn't surprised to hear Cab's voice. "Get that dog out of here."

The words were no sooner out of his mouth than the dog hurled herself into the cave. I raced across the grass and shone the lantern on the cave.

It was shallow, and the strong beam lit up the very back. Hillary was huddled against the back wall, looking terrified. Cab was closer to the front. The lantern light seemed to have temporarily blinded him. He struck out wildly at the little dog. Finally he threw his cane at her. He aimed badly and threw it too hard. It landed outside the cave, in the bushes behind me. As it hit a rock, it made a hollow, cracking sound.

"Stop it, Cab!" I shouted, afraid he'd kill Fizzy Lizzy.

Taking advantage of my momentary distraction, Hillary suddenly made a run for it. She dashed out of the cave. But before she could pass me, I stuck out my foot. She fell hard, hitting her face on a rock.

"Owwww!" she yelped in pain, but tried to stand. I dropped down beside her and pinned her hands behind her back.

Just then I heard the thump of approaching feet. "Nancy . . . is that you?" It was Officer Rees. He and two more officers burst through the underbrush. A heartbeat later Chief McGinnis lumbered into the clearing after them.

"Don't let Cab get away!" I cried.

Chief McGinnis actually laughed. "That's not going to happen. That little mutt's got him cornered." I looked up. Sure enough, sweet Fizzy Lizzy had reverted to a snarling bundle of primal hatred. She bared her teeth at Cab, but seemed to sense that cornering him was enough. "Maybe you should hire her as a police dog," I suggested. Cab finally came out of the cave with his hands up.

The officers handcuffed him and Hillary. Since

they'd found the *Belle*'s lifeboat anchored in the cove, they decided to split us all up. One group of officers, including Emily Kim, would take the police boat and bring the culprits directly back to town for booking. Chief McGinnis, Officer Rees, and I, along with Fizzy Lizzy, would take the lifeboat back to the *Belle*.

"You'd better keep that dog away from me," Cab said, as Sergeant Kim herded him back toward the path.

"Not to worry," I told him. I had borrowed a bit of rope from Officer Rees and had looped it through Fizzy Lizzy's collar for a temporary leash.

"And how about Cab's cane?" Hillary said, looking back over her shoulder. "How's he supposed to walk without it?"

Right, the cane. I remembered it had landed somewhere in the brush, a few yards from the head of the trail. I aimed my flashlight in that direction and saw something glinting against the rocks. "I found it," I said.

When I picked it up, I was sad to see the top had snapped cleanly off. But under closer inspection, I realized it had snapped *too* cleanly.

I poked through the weeds and found the carved dog's head. As I suspected, it fit neatly back into the other part of the cane. I shook the cane, and something rattled.

"I don't believe this!" I gasped.

Chief McGinnis heard me. "Now what," he grumbled, sounding annoyed.

I handed him the two parts of the cane, the bottom and the severed head. "It's hollow. Shake it . . . but be careful!" I warned.

When he shook the open end of the cane, Agnes Mahoney's emerald necklace fell right out.

"Well, I'll be!" he exclaimed. Then, with great reluctance, he looked at me and added, "Good work, Nancy."

"Want the good news, or bad news first?" I asked my friends the next day. Bess, George, and I were comfortably draped on various chairs and sofas in the conservatory of Mrs. Mahoney's house. It's one of my favorite rooms in all of River Heights. Mrs. Mahoney knew it and had invited my friends and Luther to join her and Nadine Tucker for a buffet lunch. Only Ned was missing. He was down at the *Magnolia Belle* accompanying two more groups of campers on a tour.

"I think I've heard enough bad news to last me for the next six months," Ms. Tucker spoke up. Fizzy Lizzy—renamed Delta—was comfortably curled in her lap. Ms. Tucker had decided to adopt her and was already spoiling her to death, feeding her bits of Mrs. Mahoney's elegant finger sandwiches.

"But it's better to get the bad over first," George said.

"I agree," I said. "So here goes. Even though we nabbed Cab and Hillary, her uncle and that other guy connected with the Russian mob got away. They must have seen the police boat making for Stony Lonesome Island and walked out on Hillary and Cab."

"Ah, the honor of thieves," Luther said.

"Speaking of thieves, Chief McGinnis said Hillary had cased my jewelry. But how?" Mrs. Mahoney asked.

"I don't think anyone knows. She's keeping her mouth shut on that topic, though it's likely that her uncle Jake is connected with that end of things. It's the one loose end that has me worried," I said. Then I added, "And then I found out more about Fizzy—I mean, Delta. Hillary is apparently an animal lover. . . ."

"But she's the one who doped the dog!" Mrs. Mahoney pointed out.

"Right, but she was supposed to *kill* her. She cut the dose and hoped Cab wouldn't learn she tranquilized the dog instead. Anyway, Cab had gotten Delta as a little pup from a shelter. He trained her, but was cruel and nasty about it. Apparently he abandoned Delta in that circus fire—which turns out to have been arson. Once Cab is convicted of all his crimes, he's going to be put away for a very long time."

Bess sighed. "The whole thing was so scary. Especially when he rigged that cap on the boiler. I found out he, not Dylan, had written out my shopping list for the hardware store that day." Bess frowned, but then a moment later, suddenly brightened.

"But I've got good news!" she announced. "I've got a date—with Dylan!"

"Where to? A boxing match?" George scoffed.

Bess looked prim. "No. We're going to the movies." Then she giggled. "Actually, *he* wanted to go bowling—can you imagine? The very idea of a klutzy guy with a bowling ball was ridiculous. So I insisted on the movies. And *I'm* doing the driving."

Luther looked desperate for someone to change the subject. I quickly broke in. "That's great, Bess. Hey, I hear that Hillary is giving Chief McGinnis fits! She's slipped out of her handcuffs twice, and last time she managed to make it right to the front door of the police station. Of course she keeps getting caught. So that's good. But it turns out she's not just a magician, she's a bonafide escape artist—that was one of her acts in the magic show with the circus.

"And here's my big news: the *Magnolia Belle* is staying right here in River Heights for a week—with Captain Mike at the wheel! He was working on board as an undercover FBI agent to investigate those Russian mob guys—but he found he enjoyed captaining so much, he retired, and handed the case over to a new agent. Captain Mike needs to find a new first mate and have a complete inspection made of the ship's engines. He wants to make sure that the steam buildup didn't do any permanent damage. Once it's back on its feet, Mrs. Mahoney has chartered the ship for a repeat fund-raiser cruise—and it's free for us. We're all invited!"

"It's the least I can do to thank you all, especially Nancy. That necklace is priceless. At the moment, it's safely in police hands as evidence—but as soon as I get it back, I'm bringing it to the jewelry store to get a safety latch."

Everyone cheered and lifted a glass of iced tea to toast Mrs. Mahoney.

Then George turned to me and winked. "This time around, I hope we'll just raise funds—and no detectives overboard!"